# ANTHEM OF THE DWARF KING

# ANTHEM OF THE DWARF KING

## THE ADVENTURES OF FINNEGAN DRAGONBENDER™
### BOOK THREE

CHARLEY CASE    MARTHA CARR    MICHAEL ANDERLE

LMBPN Publishing
PMB 196, 2540 South Maryland Pkwy
Las Vegas, NV 89109

First US edition, January 2020
Version 1.05, July 2021
eBook ISBN: 978-1-64202-697-9
Print ISBN: 978-1-64202-698-6

CHAPTER ONE

Finn leapt back, the tip of Mila's sword missing his chest by less than an inch. He twisted and rolled left to avoid Danica's staff. Stepping forward, he wrapped an arm around Mila's waist and pulled her against him, using her as a shield to forestall Danica's next sweeping blow.

Mila jabbed her elbow at his face, but Finn extended his arm and spun her away like a dance move. She pirouetted into the charging Danica, sending them both tumbling to the ground.

Finn loomed over the two women, his fists on his hips. He grinned. "That was better. You almost had me with the coordinated sword and staff attacks, but you projected your intentions too much."

He offered a hand to each, helping them to their feet.

"How did we project? We didn't say a thing." Mila rubbed her hip where she had fallen on the thin floor mat.

Finn picked up the dropped practice sword and staff and headed to the rack on the wall, putting the practice weapons alongside other wooden ones. "You said it all with your eyes. Remember lesson one: always watch your attacker's eyes. You glanced at Danica and gave just the slightest nod."

Mila blinked, looking baffled. "I didn't even realize. Man, it's hard to keep control in the heat of battle."

"That's why practice is key," Danica commented, going to a second rack on the wall. She grabbed a short bow and some practice arrows. "My family trained me when I was young. They gave up after discovering my healing talents and started focusing on that instead. Still, I remember my uncle telling me how important it was to go through the motions of battle so, when the time came, you could think about tactics instead of the moves." She put the arrows on a small table set aside for just such a purpose and tested the draw on the bow. She plucked an arrow up and, in a smooth action, notched, drew, and released.

The arrow zipped across the new condo's practice space and slammed into the center of a target mounted on the far brick wall. She sent three more arrows after the first, all of them hitting the target in a tight pattern.

She smiled, lowering the bow, and glanced at the open-mouthed Mila.

"I kept up the bow training," Danica said with a wry smile, "because I was already pretty good."

"That was incredible!" Mila peered downrange at the target. "I've known you for years, and I never knew you could shoot a bow, especially like this."

Danica shrugged. "I haven't practiced much since starting at the hospital. I still have my equipment in my room, but it's a little powerful for an indoor range like this."

"That's so cool." Mila slapped Danica on the ass, making the elf jump and squeal. "Atta boy, Danica. You're just full of surprises, aren't you?"

Danica laughed, handing the bow to Mila. "Want to give it a try?"

Mila nodded, and Danica went into teacher mode, showing her the basics while Finn watched. Both women were barefoot and wore matching black leggings and sports bras. They glistened with sweat from the hour-long practice, imparting them with a glow that made his heart pound faster. Danica was the 'traditionally' attractive of the two with her long legs, high cheekbones, and blonde hair sweeping down her back, but Finn couldn't help staring at Mila. To him, there was no one more attractive than the four-foot-ten, half-Mexican woman. He watched the determination on her face as Danica instructed her on how to aim. Mila was the hardest worker he had ever met, willing to try anything—at least once. Everything about her was genuine and thoughtful.

Mila was his ideal.

He wished he were worthier of her. As an exile, a black sheep, and a target of fear and ridicule from most magical species, Finn was less than desirable. She deserved a king, and he was not that.

Finn pulled his eyes from the women and admired the new addition to their home.

Two days ago, the contractors finished the remodel of the now-huge condo. Simon's and Becky's old place was larger than Mila's original condo by about a thousand square feet, and Finn had designed the new space for maximum efficiency.

The long wall in the living room of Mila's place now opened into the main area of the second condo, the area Finn called the dojo; instead of another living room and kitchen, it was one open area with the kitchen removed. Thin blue mats covered the floor for martial arts training, with recessed indirect lighting so they wouldn't be distracted by uneven glare. Racks of every type of practice and real weapons lined the walls, most of which Mila admitted she had never seen.

One of the three large bedrooms had been converted into a workshop, although it needed to be outfitted with machinery in order for it to be a proper one. It had some work benches and a few hand tools, and that was about it. The other two bedrooms were for Penny and Finn. They had their own bathrooms, with Penny's modified as a sauna with a hot and cold bath. She didn't need to shower regularly, but she enjoyed her therapeutic soaks.

The dojo's main bathroom was constructed as a locker room with a large walk-in shower with several shower-heads, along with benches and wood-trimmed cubbies to accommodate a small troop of people changing and storing their belongings while on the floor. Mila asked why they needed a locker room since they all lived there and had their own showers. Finn said he was planning ahead. He had a feeling the dojo would get plenty of use.

The additions were utilitarian, yet the woodwork was the finest Finn had seen aside from Preston's manor. Kevin and his selkies were jacks-of-all-trades. The brown-haired, otter-shifter leader had contacted Finn as soon as he had been released from the hospital, just as Finn had asked. The dwarf gave Kevin all the healing potions he needed for re-growing his amputated leg. When they met, Kevin mentioned several of his people were master carpenters who would be happy to renovate the condo. Finn agreed to use them as long as they worked quickly. Helped by magic, they completed six months of labor in two days, and Finn showered them with homemade food and a substantial bonus.

He was elated with the new place. Mila had been skeptical at first, although once she had seen the beautiful woodwork, she was sold.

Finn heard the *thwap* of a bowstring and turned to see Mila had hit the target on the outer edge—still a hit. She pumped her free fist into the air and let out a whoop of excitement.

Mila turned his way. "Did you see that?" She was all smiles, and Danica chuckled behind her.

"I did. Pretty good for a first-timer." Finn gave her a polite golf clap.

She rolled her eyes at the over-the-top patronizing. "Give me a month, and I'll be hitting bullseyes all day."

"I don't doubt it." Finn was serious, but it still made Mila laugh. "What do you guys say to some lunch? Now that you're feeling better after the ordeal with the hounds, we need to talk about the info Preston gave us."

Mila nodded, handing the bow to Danica, who set up to take a few more shots. "Sounds good, but I want to get a shower first. You should take one too. I don't want you dripping dwarf sweat in the food." She stuck her tongue out, giving him a wink.

Finn sniffed his armpit. "That's not a bad idea." He

glanced around the condo, then asked, "Have you seen Penny?"

Mila grabbed a small gym towel from the stack they kept against the wall. "She went out on the balcony about half an hour ago," she said after wiping her face.

Finn glanced out the double French doors and spied the small dragon's blue body, the red stripe down her back nearly glowing in the morning light. She was perched on the railing, eating from a box of Charleston Chews.

He stepped to the door and opened it, then stuck his head out. The sharp cold of early winter hit him in the face. Finn shivered. "Hey. You okay out here? I was about to make lunch after a shower."

Penny turned her head while keeping her body in the same position, her long neck craned over her shoulder. "Shir chi." She pointed at the distant mountains.

Finn took in the view of the city spread out below the four-story condo building and the mighty Rocky Mountains in the distance. On this clear day, the mountains were a painting, colors popping against the clear blue sky as the sun lit their faces in brilliant definition.

"It is beautiful. I've been wanting to get back out into nature myself. The location Preston gave for the *Anthem* is pretty remote. Maybe we can get a hike in while we're scouting it."

Penny bit into another mini-Chew before turning back to the view. "Shir shi shi."

Finn chuckled. "Okay, I'll let you know when lunch is ready."

CHAPTER TWO

Finn set three plates of food on the kitchen island as Danica, Mila, and Penny entered. The two women had wet hair from their showers and padded in their bare feet across the hardwood floor, showing off painted toenails under the cuffs of their comfy pajama pants. Mila had her traditional matte-black polish that matched her fingernails, while Danica sported a cherry red that glinted in the light. Penny had a smear of chocolate on her face from the Charleston Chews.

Finn joined them at the counter. He cracked open three beers and slid two to Mila and Danica. Penny dove head-first into her fried bologna sandwich. They ate in silence except for the loud crunching of potato chips.

Finn finished his sandwich before everyone else and washed it down with a few chugs of beer, then opened Mila's laptop and pulled up a map. "Preston sent over a flash drive with the info about what his people found." He wiped the corner of his mouth, making sure no crumbs were in his beard. "He said there was a high level of magical dispersion from this location two days ago. Me and Penny checked the numbers. They matched what we'd see from an exhaust plume from the *Anthem*."

"I thought..." Danica swallowed her bite of sandwich, then took a drink before continuing, "I thought the *Anthem* was destroyed by the Huldu when the Dark Star agent tried to steal it."

"That's what we all thought, but I remember this wash of red magic before the explosion." Finn raised an eyebrow. "Red magic indicates dark magic. It's possible the Dark Star was able to teleport the ship, but I can't imagine it didn't suffer some damage. Things that large are not made to be teleported long distances."

Danica's eyes went wide. "She was able to teleport an entire ship? How powerful *is* this bitch?"

"Is that bad?" Mila asked. She was not in the loop when it came to power levels. "I mean, I've seen Hermin transport a bunch of people in one go before."

"A bunch of people and an entire asteroid are two very different things." Finn finished his beer and walked to the fridge for a second. "Only someone using dark magic would have that kind of raw power. Well, there are a few creatures powerful enough to do it without resorting to dark magic, but they're pretty far and few between."

"And what makes dark magic so bad?" Mila had the look she got when she was mentally filing things for later.

Danica answered her, letting Finn open his beer and rejoin them. "Well, dark magic is super powerful, but anyone that uses it too long will be consumed by it. Some people go mad, others become evil, it depends on the user, but no one uses it for long without some serious side effect."

"And remember this is a woman that wants to start her own country," Finn added. "You can't imagine how messed up that government would be, being ruled by someone like that."

"Okay, so the *Anthem* was taken before it was destroyed." Mila narrowed her eyes. "So, we just go take it back, right? I mean, we did it before. Why can't we do it again?"

"Chi squee. Shir shee chi," Penny said, swallowing her last bite of sandwich and starting in on the chips.

"Yeah, we can't count on them being that sloppy again," Finn agreed with whatever Penny had said. "She knows what we're capable of, for the most part, and I'm sure there will be measures in place now to keep us out." He turned the computer and pointed at a lake on a satellite image of an area northwest of Denver. "I think I know what she decided to do, though. She put it at the bottom of this lake."

Mila squinted at the image. "That's Grand Lake. I used to go up there with my uncle and dad on our hunting trips. Back then it wasn't all that impressive, but now it's a destination for wealthy Denverites. Why would she put it in a lake surrounded by homes? Doesn't that seem obvious?"

"That's what I was thinking, but then Penny looked up the information on the lake itself, and it all made sense. It turns out Grand Lake is the deepest lake in Colorado that's not being used for hydroelectric. It's deep enough the *Anthem* would be hidden below the surface, and no one would suspect a thing due to changes in the flow of water."

Mila gave a half-smile. "Well, I see this as a good thing.

Even if they have the ship guarded, there is at least a chance we can get it back. You could go home."

Finn felt a pang in his heart. He had accepted this was home, but now he had a second chance to leave. Was that something Mila wanted? Was she sick of him throwing her life into chaos?

"Well, maybe," he said soberly. "But that's a pretty big if. We need to stop her from getting the ship up and running at all costs. Having the *Anthem* at the head of an attack force could spell all kinds of trouble for the Peabrains. The ship would need to be outfitted with armaments, but her shielding is far superior to anything that could be thrown at it on this planet. It would be an unstoppable machine of destruction."

"So, what do we do?" Danica wiped her lips and took a sip of beer.

"Chishee." Penny shrugged as if it were obvious.

"She's right. We need to scout the area, but the engines venting like that tell us they have a lot of work still before they get the *Anthem* in the air. With the time that gives us— a few weeks, maybe a month—we can do one thing to slow them down." Finn opened a browser tab, displaying a drawing of what looked like a tube with metal handles on either end of a glass cylinder. A yellowish-green liquid filled the cylinder. "Penny drew this up for us." The women gave Penny an appreciative look. She waved them off, although her blue skin flushed purple. "This is the fuel rod for the *Anthem*. Out in the universe, these are commonplace; every ship is powered by these in some capacity. They contain a fluid that holds concentrated magical potential. The raw magic is converted into power for propulsion and hyperdrive systems."

"Wait." Mila raised her hand. "You're telling me you guys have faster than light travel?"

Finn and Penny exchanged amused looks. "How else would we get to other galaxies?"

Mila's eyebrows were nearly to her hairline. Even Danica was surprised. "That's the holy grail of physics," said Mila. "Our scientists have been working to achieve FTL travel since we discovered relativity. Most people in the field say it's impossible."

"They're right." Finn shrugged apologetically. "Without magic, it probably is."

"What's it like?" Danica asked, her eyes bright with wonder.

Finn and Penny laughed, then realized she wasn't joking. Finn cleared his throat at her dark look. "Well, you've done it yourself. Every teleport spell you've ever used is the same as a hyperdrive, just on a smaller scale. Teleporting is instantaneous, which is faster than lightspeed."

Realization dawned on Danica. "Oh. I guess that makes it more interesting, but it's too fast to see. Is it instant in space too?"

"Pretty much." Finn raised an eyebrow at Penny so she could chime in.

The small dragon went into a long explanation, including grand gestures and spouts of flame.

"Let me guess," Mila said excitedly. "A small amount of time elapses, but you can't perceive it?"

Finn cocked his head. "Did you understand that?"

Mila rocked her head side to side. "Sort of. I mostly figured it out from her gestures, but an idea formed in my brain when she finished."

Finn glanced at Penny, who smiled wide enough he could see the teeth in the back of her mouth.

"Was I right?" Mila asked, glancing between the two.

Finn knew it required training from an early age to understand Penny, so it continued to shock him whenever Mila understood her. "You missed a few details, but that's the gist. Traveling that fast overwhelms the senses, so you can't perceive any of it until you drop back into subluminal speeds." He held up a hand and shook his head. "I'm sorry, but you can understand Penny all the sudden?"

Mila laughed. "Hardly. Being around her so much, I guess I'm figuring things out from her connotations."

"How long has that been going on?" Danica seemed as interested as Finn.

Mila gazed at the ceiling, trying to work it out. "Well, I was getting it some before the circlet burned me. Honestly, after I recovered, it does seem to be coming easier."

Finn peered at Mila, searching for a magical aura. Like every time before, she was a dead space. That didn't make sense. Understanding draconic, especially Penny's particular language, was magical on every level. Her language was unlike most languages—no direct translation of her words and gestures existed. The interpretation of those gestures and words, along with the magic that came off her, conveyed her meaning. Sure, Penny did some things anyone could translate to a point, common human gestures and such, but that was pantomiming, not speaking. If Mila comprehended her, she was interpreting Penny's magical dialect of the draconic language, which meant she had access to her magic on some level; yet, Finn couldn't see it, at least not in her aura.

Once again, he was struck by Mila. He was either too dense to figure her out, or she was so extraordinary, he didn't know what to look for.

"Okay, well, keep working on it. Penny, why don't you start some simple language lessons with her?" Finn blinked a few times to organize his thoughts. "Okay. I say we head up to Grand Lake and investigate. We need to keep a low profile, but we also need to be safe if the Dark Star has her people up there. Luckily, Preston felt the same way, so he gave us keys to his cabin." Finn pulled two metal cards about twice the thickness of a credit card from his pocket. Each card bore a complex rune etched into its surface. He set them down, and everyone inspected them like they might jump up and do a jig.

"Those are keys?" Mila asked, her brow going up.

"Yeah. The cabin is heavily warded. We need to either have one of these on us, or we need to be accepted by one of them to enter the premises. Just press your thumb to them, and they will accept you as users. He said they'd last a month, and then they need to be reset."

Taking the lead, he pressed his thumb to the metal of the top card. It flashed, making everyone flinch. Mila and Penny followed suit, the light flashing for both of them.

"I wish I could see what a cabin means to Preston Meriwether," Danica joked, getting up from the counter. "Well,

I'm off to work. I have the overnight shift, so don't wait up, you two." She gave Mila a hug and headed to her room.

"You want to watch McLintock again?" Finn suggested.

Both Mila and Penny groaned.

# CHAPTER THREE

After a long, and barely civil, conversation about the need to expand Finn's movie experience, Mila convinced him to watch *UP*. At first, he scoffed at watching a children's movie, but after the first heartbreaking ten minutes of cinema that is the backstory for *UP*, he was hooked. They ended up watching *Wall-e* next and quit only because Mila insisted they didn't burn through the entire PIXAR catalog in one sitting.

They decided on drinks and donned clothes appropriate for public viewing. Finn traded sweats for jeans and a black t-shirt, his stitched-together bomber jacket, and the brown leather shoulder holster loaded with Fragar and two healing potions, just in case. Mila lost her ducky pajama bottoms and big fluffy sweater, coming out of her room in leggings, a mock turtleneck, and knee-high boots, all black. Finn preferred a more utilitarian chunky-heeled boot, although he appreciated the exceptionally ornate leatherwork and mock laces all the way up the back of her calves.

"You ready?" she asked, pulling her short maroon leather jacket off the coat hook.

"Yeah." He held his jacket open for Penny, who snatched a fresh box of Charleston Chews from the counter and dove into the opening, then settled in her mesh hammock at the small of his back. He heard her rip the cardboard open and start chomping. "Don't leave your trash back there like last time," he warned.

A tooting reply made him roll his eyes.

Mila laughed, laying her jacket on the counter before grabbing her corset holster and wrapping it around her waist. She used the metal latches in the front to secure it, then checked that Gram and her potions were in their proper places and secured.

As she threw on her jacket, Finn felt a spike of pride. She had readied for the unexpected without him reminding her. At first, he'd worried the corset was uncomfortable, but Mila had assured him it was deceptively comfortable, although admitted she felt like she was going through a goth phase while wearing it. When he asked her to explain what a "goth phase" was, she mumbled something about a lot of black clothing and lipstick. He had seen her makeup counter in her bathroom and spied several old tubes of black lipstick, not to mention she still painted her nails a sleek matte-black.

They took the slow elevator to the lobby and stepped onto Larimer Street. Cold winter wind whipped through them, making Mila hold her thin jacket closed and give an involuntary shiver. The breeze tugged Finn's beard as he breathed the crisp air, thinking it was nice. Admittedly, he was better at regulating his body heat than Peabrains.

"Looks like it's time to break out the winter wear," Mila said, shoulders shaking.

Finn put an arm around her, sharing his body heat, and she leaned in as they started walking.

"Do you want to go back and get a heavier coat?" he asked, hitting the crosswalk button, although it was late and there were hardly any cars on the road.

She shook her head and tugged at him, forcing him to jaywalk. "Nope. We've gone too far, but you need to step on it, bub. I won't last much longer."

He picked up speed as best he could while keeping his arm around her shoulders until they were a wobbling, half-jogging mess. Finn began to laugh as he stopped on the corner at 20th street. He shrugged out of his jacket and put it around her shoulders, the huge jacket coming down to her knees.

"Here. You need this more than I do," Finn said, not finding the cold all that biting.

Penny yelped and shot from the mesh hammock on his back, landing on Mila's shoulder before crawling into the warmth of the coat and holding onto Mila's leather belt.

"Hey, as a bonus, you get a dragon to keep you toasty." Finn chuckled at Penny's annoyed glare. "Sorry, I didn't know you had become such a softy since getting to Earth."

"Chi shir shi!" She narrowed her eyes and extended the middle talon on her right hand.

Mila sniggered and closed the coat, making her look pregnant with a Penny-sized bulge. "Don't worry, Penny. You and I can stay warm together. This crazy bastard could run naked through the Arctic and be just fine."

A muffled "Chi!" let them know what she thought of that.

The night was young, but the cold front that had rolled in the previous night kept most people indoors, so no one witnessed a black van jump the curb and block their way. The side door slid open, and two men jumped out before the van even stopped. They held pistols and wore black ski masks, and the rest of their tactical gear looked like something from a catalog for mercenaries.

Finn pushed Mila behind him as he reached for Fragar and lowered his center of gravity for a fight.

The men spread apart to get multiple angles on Finn and leveled their pistols. "Hand up, buddy," the left one said with menace. "You two are coming with us one way or the other."

The other man flashed a toothy smile through his ski mask. "We don't know who you people are, but the bounty on your heads will put us firmly with the big boys."

"Keep it professional, Jim," the left one growled.

Jim glared through his mask at his partner. "Don't fucking use my name, idiot."

"What's it matter?" Left Guy stepped toward Finn, gun pointed at his head.

Finn had checked the Dark Star bounty status several times with the phone ripped from their first assassin's pocket at the hospital. Last he checked, the price was five million for his capture or one million for his body. Mila had a half a million, dead or alive, on her. So far, no mention of Penny; not including her was a huge mistake on the Dark Star's part, but he figured mentioning a dragon kind of ruled out Peabrain assassins. The Dark Star was going for quantity over quality.

"What's it matter? I don't know, *George*. What *does* it matter?"

Finn's vision reddened around the edges and his heart rate climbed. Behind him, he heard Mila whisper the power word for her armor.

The two mercs continued arguing, although George kept his cool better than Jim, who waved his pistol around as they squabbled. "This was supposed to be a quick snatch and grab, but you had to go and blow our cover."

A few people across the street stopped to stare.

George ground his teeth. "Will you shut the fuck up and zip-tie this giant? Use two ties; I don't want him breaking free in the van."

"You fucking zip-tie him. I have him covered," Jim argued, not covering Finn in the least since his arms were in the air.

"Jim, you fucking braindead son of a—"

Finn leaped forward. He didn't bother with a weapon.

George turned, eyes wide. Finn's massive hand engulfed his head, lifted the man into the air, and slammed him into the van through the still-open doors. George hit the steel bed with a loud *thump*, and his body went limp.

Jim screeched and pointed his gun at Finn's back.

Finn went to summon a pillar of rock to knock Jim back, but his rage kept the magic just out of reach.

A third merc shouted, fumbling for something as he sat in the van's driver's seat.

Finn spun toward Jim as a blue and red streak shot from Mila's coat and latched onto Jim's face. Penny let out a tiny roar, and Jim stumbled and swung the butt of his pistol at her back. At the last second, she jumped away, and Jim smashed his own nose. It sprayed blood, and he screamed.

Mila shoulder-checked Jim as he clutched his face, sending him toward Finn, who tossed him into the van. The man slammed into the interior's far wall and crumpled to the floor on top of the unconscious George.

The glass of the passenger side window exploded inward as Penny hit it with a superheated flame. She slid into the van and flared her wings in the driver's face.

"Leave," Finn growled, his eyes dark with menace. "Don't come back. Ever."

The merc looked from the dragon, smoke and flame roiling from her clenched teeth, and then at Finn. He nodded and threw the van into reverse. The tires squealed on the sidewalk, and the van rocked off the curb and into the street. No one was coming, so the van peeled out, sending snow and slush up in a rooster tail, then sped down the street and around the corner.

Penny landed on Finn's shoulder and placed her hand on his cheek. She cooed.

It took a few seconds before Finn could think clearly, his rage abating from her soothing magical touch.

"Are you okay?" Mila approached cautiously and slipped her hand into his.

He nodded, eyes closed, and gave her hand a squeeze, then opened his eyes and smiled. "I think I could use a drink."

CHAPTER FOUR

F inn and Mila bellied up to the long oak bar inside The Refinery. Danny, the bartender, noticed Finn's dour expression and served their usual, a double whiskey and a beer and a G&T, without being asked. He also gave them a bowl of peanuts and moved to the far end of the bar, picking up a paperback and sticking his nose in it.

Considering the cold and late hour on a weekday, about six other people paired off at the various booths in quiet conversation, the soft pop music was playing just loud enough to be heard without being obtrusive.

Penny climbed out of Mila's bomber jacket and onto the bar. She stretched out her arms like she was about to dive into a pool, then slipped into the bowl of peanuts, munching loudly.

Mila hung their jackets on the back of her stool and climbed into the seat. She crossed her arms on the bar and put her head down. "This has got to stop," she said, her voice muffled in her sleeves. She raised her head and glanced at Finn. "I thought it was all over when we got the hounds back. I mean, I knew it wasn't, but I guess I wished it was."

Finn threw back the double shot in one gulp, then put the glass down and enjoyed the smoky flavor before answering, "Yeah. The only way to stop them is to either get our names off the site or stop the Dark Star. Since she can just put the bounty back up, looks like we need to stop her."

"Chi chir." Penny lounged in her bowl.

"I don't think moving will do the trick, Penny," Mila responded. "Besides, you warded the condo. It's safe enough."

Finn raised an eyebrow. Mila didn't seem to notice she'd understood Penny. Even the dragon was shocked, although less than Finn. She had been trying to teach Mila how to understand her, but they hadn't had much headway except for the occasional blip, like earlier during lunch.

"Speaking of," Finn slowly said, back to speed after Mila's spontaneous translation. "Penny, I think we need to reinforce the wards. If we get any hitmen with real magical abilities, we'll need a more robust protection grid. Do you have anything more you can do?"

She thought about it and nodded. "Shee." A ring of smoke drifted from her nostril. He didn't ask her to elaborate; wards were her job, and he didn't know how to craft them for shit.

"Damn it." Mila discerned a smear of blood on her hand.

"Holy shit, are you okay?" Finn reached behind the bar and grabbed a small handful of napkins.

"Yeah, I must have cut my hand when I charged that

guy." She pressed the napkins to her palm and applied pressure. "I'm going to go to the bathroom and clean this up. It looks pretty shallow."

"Take a healing potion." Finn reached for a vial tucked into his pouch on his holster.

She slipped off the stool, waving off his offer. "I'm not taking a thousand-dollar potion for a tiny cut. I'll clean it up. It's not bleeding anymore."

"Well, at least take Penny. I don't think there are any more of those mercs around, but better safe than sorry."

Mila waved for Penny to come. "I guess we can have a little girl time while I clean up."

Penny slipped out of the bowl, shaking peanut dust off like a dog that had just come out of the bath. She leapt to Mila's shoulder and Finn watched them go, appreciating Mila's shapely behind, then shook his head and turned back to his drink.

"Hey, man. I know how that goes."

Finn nearly jumped out of his seat.

An old man occupied the stool beside him. The best word Finn could find to describe him was "threadbare." The man's thin frame was draped with a large, heavy coat that looked like it had been made out of several other coats. A long red wool scarf hung around his neck, one end trailing to the floor, where it crumpled in a pile. He had long white hair pulled into a ponytail that hung past his shoulders and a thick white beard, the hair contrasting with his dark skin.

Finn took him for a homeless man who had wandered in off the street, yet something about his eyes told Finn something that wasn't true. "I'm sorry, what?"

The old man held out a leathery hand. "Name's Rolf. Rolf Williamson. Pleasure to finally meet you, Finn."

Finn raised an eyebrow but took the offered hand and shook it. He wondered if this might be an odd attempt to collect the bounty on him, so he extricated his hand after one pump.

"How is it you know my name, old-timer?" Finn's hand itched to reach for the folded axe at the small of his back.

Rolf chuckled. "Don't worry. I'm not here for any bounty, man." He held up a glass of bubbly water. "I just like the seltzer here. I think they put extra bubbles in it." He winked before taking a sip and smacking his lips.

"That's great and all, but it doesn't answer my question, Rolf. How do you know who I am?" Finn felt the rage at the back of his skull like a coiled viper.

Rolf pursed his lips and squinted at the ceiling. "That's the question we all ask ourselves, isn't it? How do we know who we are? Ya know? Like on the inside, who are we?"

Finn frowned. This guy was not an assassin in a clever disguise. He was just some old stoner. He cleared his throat. "No, I asked, how do *you* know who I am?"

Rolf's eyes widened, then he snickered. "Sorry, man. I thought you were getting into the heavy stuff right away."

"'The heavy stuff?'"

Rolf bobbed his head. "Yeah, man. You know—life, love, why we exist. The *heavy* stuff."

"Are you high?" Finn felt comfortable this old nut couldn't be dangerous. He was far too chill.

"Almost always, man." He gave Finn a big smile full of perfectly white teeth. "You should give it a try. That's the whole reason I moved here. They saw the need and released the weed. Best ten years of my life."

Finn grinned at the stupid rhyme. "I don't think getting high is the answer right now. I have a little too much going on."

Rolf nodded. "I figured you were going to say that. Shame, man. It really helps with the rage."

Finn focused on the old man, suspicious again. "The rage? What would an old-timer like you know of the rage?"

"We'll get to that in a minute." Rolf took another sip of seltzer water. "I've been watching you, man. Ever since word on the street got to me about a dwarf, I knew I had to check you out." He laughed, the sound a melodic slow beat. "It took me a minute to figure out you weren't some short ugly dude with a giant axe and a beard. Well, I guess the beard and the axe are true, but pretty cool when he turns out to be six-five and good- looking."

"Yeah, what's up with that?" Finn frowned. "I watched *The Lord of the Rings* and busted a gut laughing at the 'dwarves.'"

Rolf laughed. "Yeah, that's about what I expected to find. Turns out dwarves aren't exactly a loved species among the magicals. When the last of you died out, they changed the narrative. A spite thing, I guess. Man, you people must have really pissed a lot of folks off for them to besmirch your entire race."

Finn frowned harder. "I might not like the outcome, but I can't blame them. Most dwarves are insufferable. That's why I left in the first place." Finn cocked an eyebrow. "Wait, you know about magicals? How?"

Rolf wiggled his fingers, and a glitter of golden light

drifted from them. The smell of heated steel filled the area, then a small bubble formed in the bowl of peanuts before popping and transporting a handful of nuts into Rolf's hand.

"I'm one of 'em, man." He narrowed his eyes. "I thought you were all smart and stuff. Don't princes get, like, special education?"

"You seem to know a lot about me, Rolf Williamson. And you don't seem to be telling me much in return."

The old man tossed a few nuts into his mouth and chewed, talking with his mouth full. "Well, let's remedy that. You wanna hear my story? It might help you out."

Finn glanced toward the restrooms and saw no sign of Mila or Penny. "Sure. Guess I have a few minutes."

"Right on, man."

# CHAPTER FIVE

R olf wiggled his fingers, and the smell of hot steel filled Finn's nostrils again. "Let me set the scene, man," he said, in a mysterious stoner-tainted drawl. "The year is 1969. The war has been going on for fifteen years roughly, depending on who you ask."

The wet smell of vegetation and rain replaced the steel scent. A bubble formed close to the bar, out of sight of passersby, and Finn and Rolf leaned in. The translucent bubble filled with white fog that resolved into thick jungle foliage. Finn discerned what he assumed was a soldier. The view swung around, and he made out five more of them in green fatigues, their helmets camouflaged with bits of local vegetation. They had black grease smeared on their faces, covering tight expressions. Each man clutched a rifle and wore a grenade belt. The view swung the other way and revealed four more apprehensive soldiers.

"I was the squad's sergeant." Rolf sobered with the retelling. "We were ordered into a village that had been taken by the enemy. No civies, just enemy. No one to look out for, kill-'em-all kinda thing. We had reports only five of them were there, their reinforcements still an hour away. It was supposed to be easy."

Rolf displayed a haunted look as the soldiers moved forward. Finn realized he was watching one of Rolf's memories. The view was his, but its clarity was beyond what most memories could produce, which meant it was one he often revisited. Finn experienced a pang of empathy. He had a few memories like that tucked in the back of his mind, too.

Rolf emerged from his dark thoughts, snapping his fingers and freezing the image. "Before we get into this, I need to give you a bit of backstory." He smiled and took a huge gulp of seltzer, making a pained face as it foamed down his throat. "Spicy!"

He thumped his chest a few times. "Sorry. Backstory. Ever since I was a kid, I'd have bouts of anger. My parents would send me to my room. It was a frustrating situation. I'd get mad, and they would send me to my room, I'd get madder at the injustice, you know? Like a never-ending loop of rage."

Finn's brows raised. It sounded similar to his childhood, minus the being sent to his room. The rage was very familiar.

"You're a berserker," Finn stated.

Rolf nodded. "Of course, no name for it back then, before I awoke. I was just an angry guy. So, I did the only thing I could at the time; I joined the military. I figured they would know what to do with me and, boy, did they. The first sergeant I pissed off was a ticket to the frontline. And I stayed there, beating the odds, taking bullets that should have killed me but just laid me up for a few weeks. You know, man, I've been shot twenty-seven times. That's got to be some kind of record. They kept trying to send me home, but I'd refuse." He waved a dismissive hand to clear the air. "Anyway, all that to say, I know about rage. Hell, most guys I served with knew about it. They'd get me all riled up and turn me loose."

He snapped his fingers, and the view in the bubble started up again.

Finn watched as they moved into a small village, about five or six huts made of grass and wood, not much to talk about. The village seemed empty, but the soldiers at Rolf's side didn't ease up. Keeping low, they spread out, rifles ready.

The tinny voice of one of the soldiers filtered out of the bubble. "Sarge, I don't think they're—"

The tiny bubble lit up with gunfire from the huts. Soldiers scattered, letting loose with their rifles. Finn watched as Rolf gunned the enemy down, killing one and moving to the next. Finn heard Rolf's heavy breathing climbing in tempo as the rage took hold. Rolf emptied his gun and, instead of reloading, he grabbed the hot barrel and held it like a club, smoke coming from his hands where the hot metal burned his flesh. Rolf charged a hut while the occupant fired round after round at him, yet he kept going and kicked the door in. The wood exploded inward, splitting down the middle, ripped from the hinges. The shooter at the window swung the tip of his smoking gun at Rolf. He never had a chance to pull the trigger. Rolf growled and used his makeshift club to bash the man's skull.

Finn saw himself in the savage actions. He watched as

Rolf found two more targets and beat them to death. Bursting out of the last hut, Rolf howled like an animal, hands and arms covered in blood. He searched for another target, but the village was quiet.

"Where are your men?" Finn asked in a soft whisper.

The pain in Rolf's eyes told the answer.

In the bubble, Rolf found the first of his fallen men, burned to a crisp; far worse than should have been possible in the time Rolf went from hut to hut. There was another, burned like the first, mere ash in human form. He discovered more, and his roars of anguish echoed through the jungle.

"This is it, man," Rolf said low. "The moment it all changed."

Laughter emerged from the bubble. Soldier Rolf turned and saw a man in the middle of the ruined village amid the dead, his hand raised, a bubble the size of a basketball floating above his palm. The man said something, but Finn didn't understand the language. Rolf roared and charged. The man threw the bubble and it burst into a white and orange ball of fire, filling the air with smoky tendrils.

The flames engulfed Rolf, yet he kept charging, the magical heat not touching him in his berserker state. He burst through the flames, swinging his rifle club high, and bashed the wizard's face over and over. The memory faded as Rolf howled. The bubble went hazy gray, the smell of jungle and blood fading with the image, then dissolving.

Rolf sucked his teeth, then finished off the seltzer water in two long gulps. "That was the first time I ever saw magic, man. It broke something loose in my head, you know? Once I came down from my rage, I stumbled to base. They kept me in the hospital for a month, figuring I'd gone buggy. The report said my men were ambushed and killed in a firefight. I never mentioned the wizard."

He took a deep breath and waggled his fingers, refilling his seltzer water with a quick spell.

"I get how that would have been hard," Finn said. "I take it they sent you home after that?"

Rolf glanced at him with a smile on his face. "No. I'd be dead if they had sent me home. No, man, what I showed you was just the beginning." He took a deep breath and leaned back, folding his arms over his chest. "During that month in the hospital, I wasn't just moping around. I had a mission. That thing that broke loose? It was my peabrain waking up. I sensed the magic inside me, and I knew I could make it come out. I worked in secret in that hospital bed, honing the craft through sheer willpower."

Finn's eyes widened. "That's astonishing. Most people need at least a basic lesson in manipulation to manifest even the smallest spell. You just willed it?"

"Oh, yeah, man." Rolf smiled, gloating, then his face fell. "I also failed to learn the most important lesson. I failed to understand the rage tucked that power away, out of reach when you need it most. Like in that fight you just had on the street—yeah, man, I saw you guys—a simple spell could have dealt with the second merc, but you had to rely on your friends. Nothing wrong with relying on friends, but it shouldn't put you and them in danger, you know? That lesson was the hardest."

"What happened?" Finn was sure this story didn't have a happy ending.

"I began using my magic to fight the enemy. What do you know, I'm a wizard, Harry!" He barked a laugh.

Finn furrowed his brow. "Harry?"

Rolf looked taken aback. "Harry Potter, man? You're no fun. Anyway, the magic was just the edge I needed to keep my men safe, and I could get spells off without any of them seeing a thing. I didn't fall into the rage for months. But all good things come to an end."

He sobered before continuing. "Eventually we got into a fight where I was flanked. Had to go hand-to-hand with these two guys because I had gotten too cocky. The rage took me fast. While deep in the bloodlust, I caught sight of an armored transport rolling up, but my men didn't notice. I tried to send off a spell to take out the transport, but my magic failed, man. The rage kept my powers out of reach. I watched more of my men die, only this time, it was because I didn't understand my limitations."

Finn nodded. He was all too aware of a berserker's constraints. "As a child, I was taught to never rely on magic in battle. Berserkers and spell-slingers are like oil and water."

Rolf smiled a cheeky smile. "Yeah, that's what I figured out. Thing is, I was wrong."

"The fuck is that?" someone yelled close to the bathrooms. Finn looked around.

A patron had run into Mila coming out of the women's room with Penny sitting on her shoulder. The man who had shouted had backed away at the sight of the little dragon, who put on her most innocent face.

"Don't worry." Mila held up her hands in a calming

motion. "She's a *draco volans* lizard. Exotic, but nothing to be worried about."

The guy cleared his throat, his face turning red. "Sorry, it was a little shocking." He leaned in and smiled. "What's her name?"

"Penny." Mila glanced at the dragon. "Say hello, Penny."

Penny gave the guy a wave and a toothy grin.

The guy flinched and waved back.

Mila laughed and headed toward the bar.

Finn turned to introduce Rolf to her, but the old man was nowhere to be seen.

"Where did he go?" Finn asked, moving the stool to the side and checking the floor as if the man could have been hiding behind it. Even his glass was gone.

"What guy?" Mila asked, climbing onto her stool.

"The old guy."

Mila raised an eyebrow. Penny mimicked the expression from her shoulder. "Uh, what old guy? The only old guy I see is you, big guy." She socked him in the shoulder.

Finn frowned. He could still smell the faint hot steel of Rolf's magic; that, and the strong scent of weed.

## CHAPTER SIX

"Hey, Danny." Finn raised a finger to get the bartender's attention.

Danny lowered his paperback, nodded, and put the book on the back shelf after dogearing his page. Grabbing another rocks glass, he filled it with a double shot of Finn's preferred whiskey.

"'Ere ya go, Finnegan." He noticed the first glass of whiskey was still half full and set the second glass beside it. "Double fistin', eh? Atta boy." He dropped a conspiratorial wink.

"Thanks, Danny. You ever seen the old-timer I was just talking to?"

Danny's eyebrow crept up his forehead. "Whatcha on aboot now? Yer de only gob at de bar these last ten minutes."

Finn frowned, then held his glass up in a toast. "Never mind. Thanks, Danny."

Danny nodded and turned to Mila and Penny. "Need a refresh, Mila?"

Mila glanced at Penny, who shook her head. "Nope, all good. Thanks."

Danny glanced from Mila to Penny and back before smiling and walking away. Finn heard him mutter under his breath as he flipped a bar rag onto his shoulder. "Dat fookin lizard. I donna get hipsters." He grabbed his paperback and settled against the counter.

Mila shoulder-bumped Finn. "You okay?"

He watched Penny climb into her bowl of nuts before shoving a handful in her mouth. "Just had a weird talk with some random guy." He smiled. "How are you doing? Are your headaches gone?"

She squinted an eye and shrugged. "I still get them, but they're better than that first couple of days. It feels like when you have a hard workout, and it takes a few days before your muscles are back to normal. The pain is less, but it's still there every once in a while. If I have any magic in me, it's hiding well. Danica has taken me through a few exercises to check for magical abilities, but I think I might be a dud." She tapped the side of her skull. "Just a normal boring human up here."

Finn forced a smile. "You know that's not true. All Peabrains can use magic."

"Yeah, but Danica said because we all have the ability, it doesn't mean we all *can* awaken." She slapped him on the back. "Sorry, Finn. Looks like you're stuck with a nonmagical."

Finn puffed air out of his nose in a silent laugh. "You are a lot of things, Dr. Winters, but normal is not one of them. Speaking of, are you still able to communicate with insects? You know, like a *normal* human?"

She snorted before taking a sip of her G&T. "Okay, maybe not normal, but you, Danica, and Penny all confirmed *that's* not magic. We don't know what it is, but you can't detect any magic when I do it, so…"

"True." He tipped his beer back and took a swig. "But you can still do it?"

"Yeah. I made a deal with a spider today. She wanted to stay in my room for the winter. I told her okay, but she'd have to do her hunting on the balcony because pickings are slim in our place. She said that was fine and would be out as soon as the thaw came."

Finn cocked his head. "Isn't that advanced compared to what you can get out of them? I thought you said communication was one-way, you telling them what to do and gesturing to communicate."

"I guess it is more robust than normal. Now that I think about it, it was more of a conversation than I'm used to, but it made sense." She raised a questioning eyebrow. "What do you think it means?"

Finn considered. "Well, if talking to insects is a natural ability, it would make sense that if the circlet did some irreparable damage to your magic center and magic was interfering with that ability…" He left the rest unsaid and shrugged.

"Shir chi chi, shee," Penny added, having followed the conversation. Her arms were draped over the lip of the bowl as she laid on her back, her tail flicking back and forth.

"I mean, I guess so." Finn conceded her point.

Mila frowned as she looked from Penny to Finn. "You guess so what? What did she say?"

Finn opened his mouth, then closed it. He glanced at Penny, and she shrugged. "You didn't understand her?"

Mila snorted. "How would I have understood her? I don't speak draconic, remember? I mean, I get a few things, but that was too much."

"But you understood her earlier."

Mila's brows rose. "I did? That's news to me."

"When we first got here…" He held up a hand and shook his head. "Never mind. She said maybe it's the opposite, and the trauma from the circlet may have woken you up a bit. And communicating with insects *is* magic. We just don't recognize it."

"Is that possible? I thought magic was energy you could harness in different ways. That's how Danica describes it."

Finn finished his whiskey and set the glass at the back of the bar so Danny could see he'd finished it. He sucked in a breath, organizing his thoughts. "She's right. Magic is energy. As a dwarf, I use the same energy an elf or Peabrain uses, I just use it differently, all the way back to the source."

"What do you mean, 'back to the source?'" Mila's scientific training kicked in. She leaned toward him.

"Think of magic as electricity."

Mila nodded, following the analogy.

"Okay, so you have a lamp that needs to be lit," he continued. "When it lights up on that electricity could be from many processes; you could have a steam generator or a hydro-electric dam or a nuclear reactor. They all have the same end result, which is lighting the lamp, but how they get there is incompatible with one another. If you stick plutonium in a dam, it does nothing but irradiate the water, like if you pour water on the fire heating the steam engine, which would just put it out."

Mila considered, then nodded. "Okay, I follow, but you can always measure electricity—or magic. Why can't you see what I'm doing is magical or not?"

"Well, this is where the analogy breaks down. It works because most magicals use the same magical energy. Like everyone uses electricity across the globe, you have to remember there are more kinds than electricity. There's gravity, which uses potential and kinetic energy. There's even zero-point energy out in the universe; we can't measure it, but that's a whole other bag of kittens. All magic is energy, but not all energy is the same. A few beings we know of don't use the same magic as everyone else, but they're rare and seldom associate with anyone but their own."

Mila took a drink, thinking it over. "What beings?"

"What?" Finn froze with his beer halfway to his lips.

"What types don't use the same source?"

Finn set his beer down without drinking and cleared his throat. "Some elder dragons figured out how to tap into other sources." He raised the beer again and said, "Also angels and demons." He began drinking, not looking at her.

Mila goggled at him. "I'm sorry, angels? Demons? Those are real?"

Finn finished his beer. Issues with religion seemed to get Peabrains in a tizzy. "Those are the best words for them. They're not the same as all the religious connotations, just two races that evolved with a different understanding of magical forces in the universe. No need to worry, none of them were on *Earth* when it started its journey."

"If none were here, why are there so many myths?" She rolled her hand and shrugged. "I mean, I get that the original passengers knew about them, but why all the myths if they were just another race?"

Penny snickered, drawing a cocked eyebrow from Mila. "Squee, chi chi!"

Finn agreed with her. "Yeah, they aren't 'just another race.' They're more powerful than that. Plus, in the past, they fought a war that makes the Dwarven-Troll War look like playtime, and that's been going on for a few thousand years."

"You're telling me these angels and demons are so badass that Peabrains remembered them even after they forgot about magic?"

Finn nodded. "Pretty much." He saw the worry in her eyes and took her hand in his. "I'm sure it has nothing to do with you. You're a mystery. We'll figure it out given time."

She smiled. "You're right. Nothing to worry about."

Finn decided on a subject change. "How do you feel about your combat training? I know it's only been a few days, but you seem to be taking to it."

She brightened and squeezed his hand before letting go to grab her drink. "I suppose it helps that my teacher's pretty good." She winked and took a sip.

"I agree. Not about the teacher part so much, but that you're doing well. Remember, it takes years to train your body to react without thought. Don't go charging in simply because you learned the proper technique to throw a solid punch."

Mila rolled her eyes. "Don't worry. I'll let you take the first hit every time. Maybe we should get me a gun. You know, so I can be of some use."

As Finn chuckled, an idea came to him. He folded and filed it for later.

# CHAPTER SEVEN

"How are we gonna deal with the *Anthem* being at the bottom of a lake?" Mila mumbled. She kept fuzzy-eyed contact with Finn as she took another sip of her third G&T. She held up a finger to forestall his answer. "A lake, I might add, my good sir, that is *froshen* over by now. Oh! And has a town and houses surrounding it."

Finn chuckled at her flushed cheeks and slurred words. He could tell she was well into buzzed and knocking on drunk's door. From his months with Mila, Finn was accustomed to her levels of drunkenness. She didn't do it often, and never without someone to monitor her, but she let loose occasionally. Mostly her imbibing was confined to their fluffy couch. Stage one, she loosened her shoulders and yammered more than usual. She called it her "social stage."

In the second stage, she got affectionate with everyone around. Nothing inappropriate, but she would hug her friends with zeal and found a reason to slap Danica or Finn on the ass and yell "good game!" or some other clichéd "attaboy" phrase.

Stage three shifted from stage two; it went from affectionate to assertive, which took the form of whipping her socks off, plopping her feet in Finn's lap, and demanding foot rubs. In a social setting, she ducked under Finn's or Danica's arm and put it around her shoulders. Any stage beyond the third was more abstract the drunker she got until Finn carried her to bed before she made a real fool of herself.

Right now, he judged her at early stage two, although that would move along to foot rubs by the time they got home. Truth be told, he didn't mind stage three.

Finn sucked his teeth and gave her a manic grin. "Well, having the ship at the bottom of a lake is a problem. Either she put the ship in the lake because it was a convenient place to hide a small asteroid, or she did it to combat me."

Mila pulled her legs up onto the stool and got into a kneeling position. She was short, so sitting on her legs only boosted her enough to be as tall as an average person. She often sat like that when the bar was crowded, so she could see past the people around her.

"How does it bein' in a lake combat you?" Her eyes went wide. "You 'fraid of water or somethin'?"

Finn laughed. "No, nothing like that."

"Shir shee!" Penny piped up from her empty bowl. Finn had ordered her a whiskey when they got their second round, and she was halfway through the drink, but a high level of snark was the only sign the brown liquid affected her.

Mila snorted a laugh. "You *are* afraid of water!" She held

out her fist to Penny who bumped it before lifting the bucket-sized glass to her lips and taking a gulp.

"I don't like it, but I'm not *afraid* of it," he protested. "I have a healthy respect for large bodies of water is all. That's not the point. The Dark Star wouldn't know about that anyway, but she knows I'm a dwarf. Dwarves use earth magic. There's not much earth in a lake, at least not close enough for me to do anything with it."

"So, ya think she did it on purpose? What a bitch." Mila sneered as she finished her drink.

"I'm sure we established that when she started sending assassins and mercenaries after us." Finn grinned at Mila's over-the-top indignation. "But to answer the question, I was thinking of asking Kevin if any of his selkies could come along. Their otter forms should have no problem with the cold water, plus they could slip past any observation without too much trouble."

Mila bent at the waist, folded her hands in her lap, and rested her chin on the bridge his forearm made from his elbow to the bar top. She looked up at him with big brown eyes for a second. "That's a great idea," she said, her head bobbing up and down since her chin was resting on his arm.

The move was so weird that Finn didn't know what to do. She put her weight into the lean on his arm, so he didn't want to move it, although it was an odd thing for her to do. He stared down at her, his face a mask of confused amusement.

Mila laughed, sat up, and tilted her empty glass to get an ice cube. She started crunching it.

"Are you drunker than I think you are?" Finn asked, not sure what to make of her goofiness.

"I'm great." She waggled her eyebrows at him. "How you doin'?"

"Uh, I'm good."

She whipped her phone out and began to compose a text, flashing him over-the-top looks like she was doing something she didn't want him to see.

Finn peered at Penny, who had an eye ridge raised as far as it would go. She shrugged.

Mila dropped her phone on the bar like it was a mic and she'd just won a rap battle. "*Boom*. Text sent."

"Text to who?" Finn was lost. "Are you having a stroke? Do you smell burnt toast?"

Her face split into a wide grin. "No. I'm just having fun. Come on, man, loosen up. Don't you ever want to do whatever sometimes? Just act like an idiot because it freaks your friends out?"

Finn shook his head. "I've never had friends before... well, besides Penny. But we are always working. You're the first friend I've ever had."

Mila sobered. Her face fell into a pout, and her eyes misted over. She stared at him, her bottom lip working as she tried not to cry. She stared so long Finn became uncomfortable.

"Uh, I mean, it's fine. Back at the palace when I was growing up, I spent a lot of time with the weapons master. Being a berserker made it hard to keep people around, at least until I was old enough to get a handle on it. The weapons master was a good guy, but—"

Mila threw her arms around him and buried her face in

his neck. "Holy shit, Finn. The only person you considered a friend growing up was the guy who taught you how to kill people? What parents do that to their son?"

Finn put his arm around her, patting her back to comfort her. He could feel wetness where her tears were soaking into his beard.

"As a berserker, I was useful as a weapon, but that was about it." He grimaced at old memories that surfaced unbidden. "That was one reason I left. Among many."

Mila's phone buzzed on the bar top.

Finn felt her kiss his neck before pulling away. She wiped her eyes with the back of her hand, then gave him a wet stare. "Well, you have a friend now. Hell, you have quite a few friends." She held up the phone and showed him there was a text from Kevin. "Including the ones you're gathering along the way."

She opened the phone and scanned the text, summing it up for Finn. "He says he has some selkies who would be perfect for the job. He'll send them over in the morning so we can talk to them." She clicked the phone asleep and dropped it again.

"That's good news." It surprised Finn how easy it was to get Kevin to help. "I figured I would have to convince him. He's protective of his people."

She nodded. "True, but he knows the value in experience, it would seem." She yawned, then fell forward onto his arm. She slipped her arms around his and gave his bicep a tight hug. "Let's go home. I'm ready to change into pajamas and lie around on the couch. We can watch a movie with the Duke."

Finn smiled at the top of her head, giving her shoulder

an affectionate pat before holding up a finger to get the bartender's attention. "We'll close out, Danny."

"Shee squee." Penny climbed out of the empty bowl and shook off peanut dust.

"Squee chi shrik?"

It surprised Finn that Penny would want to work on the wards tonight since she didn't like the cold that much. Not to say she couldn't combat it with her internal fire, she just didn't care for it. "I figured you'd wait until morning when the sun's out."

She shook her head. "Chi chi, shir."

"I agree they need to be bolstered, but the chances of someone coming along who can get past what you have up now are slim."

Penny patted Mila's arm, smiling at the half-sleeping woman. "Chi."

Finn gazed at Mila, who had her eyes closed. She was clinging to him. "You're right. Better safe than sorry. I'll have some hot coffee waiting."

Penny gave him a narrow gaze and shook her head. "Shir shee."

Finn laughed. "Okay, hot cocoa."

# CHAPTER EIGHT

Finn awakened when he heard a knock on the front door. Like most soldiers, he was trained to ignore normal sounds and only hear the others. The sounds of Mila practicing in the dojo hadn't even made him twitch, but he bolted upright at the soft knocking sound.

He rubbed his eyes as he listened to Mila's bare feet pad across the condo. Then she opened the door, which was followed by cheerful greetings between her and two others.

Finn sighed and searched through the pile of clean laundry on the foot of his bed for jeans and a t-shirt. He struggled into them, then rubbed the sleep from his eyes as he glanced at the clock—7:24 AM.

"How the hell are you up? And practicing?" Finn mumbled at the door. He hadn't even been close to drunk, and he was struggling. Mila had drunk a beer after they'd come home and passed out on the couch as Finn rubbed her feet, then he'd carried her to her room and tucked her in before going to bed himself. It irked him she could get up as early as she did, let alone after being hammered the night before.

He shuffled across the carpet and took a deep breath, enjoying the dark and quiet of his room before pulling his door open.

As he stepped into the dojo's open area, the bright light of the sun accosted him, beaming from the ceiling windows that ran around the balcony. Finn grunted. His vision adjusted, and he stretched his neck. He enjoyed sleeping in a bed again, instead of the couch, like he'd been doing since he had arrived.

"Finn? You want some coffee?" Mila called from the kitchen.

Finn cleared his throat before he could get any volume, sleep still hanging on. "Yeah, coffee would be great."

He strode across the blue mats, his bare feet making a swishing sound as he went, and came into the living room. Mila stood behind the island, dropping a handful of Charleston Chews into a mug before pouring seaming black liquid from a French press into it. Finn smiled. She knew what he liked.

She was dressed in tights and a sports bra, and he discerned a light sheen of sweat on her shoulders. Two figures he didn't recognize sat at the island; he figured they must be the selkies. They turned at his approach, and it surprised him to see that they were almost identical to one another, one a boy, the other a girl. They didn't look like they could be a day over twenty. Both had short brown hair; the boy's was cut in a similar fashion to Finn's—long on top and buzzed at the sides. The girl had the same cut, although more feminine.

They gave him matching smiles and waves, then got up and approached, the boy holding out his hand. "Hello, Mr. Dragonbender. I'm Ronan, and this is my sister, Regan. We're excited to help you."

Finn shook both their hands. "Call me Finn. 'Mr. Dragonbender' is far too much of a mouthful. Nice to meet you both." He gave them an appraising going over. "How old are you two, if you don't mind me asking?"

"Eighteen," Regan said and flashed a bright smile. "Don't worry, we grow up fast. Me and Ronan have been working for the family for a few years now."

Mila came over, handing Finn his cup of coffee. "Doing what?"

Finn took the cup and inhaled, smelling roasted nuttiness with a hint of chocolate and nougat.

The twins glanced at one another. Ronan took the lead. "Many things…" he started vaguely, "Mostly running errands, although lately we've been doing a little…uh, let's call it 'finding things that have fallen off of trucks.'"

Mila narrowed her eyes. "Stealing?"

Both twins waved their hands in front of them and shook their heads. "No, nothing like that," Regan protested.

"More like making deals with people who find stuff," Ronan added. "We don't have the luxury of asking where it came from. It's expensive to take care of a whole clan and live in the city. We do what we can to get by."

"I get it." Finn said and had another sip. "I've been there. Me and Penny once had to make a deal for a stolen fuel rod to get off-planet before we were chopped up and served in soup. The Sisters of Gorlat do not mess around." He gave everyone a knowing glance, but they all had no idea what he was talking about. He sighed. "So, do you two know how to handle yourselves in a fight...*if* it comes down to it?"

They nodded and Regan answered, "Kevin makes it a point for us to know some martial arts and know which end of a pistol is which, and we hunt every year. Cheapest way to fill a freezer with good meat. So, yeah, I think we both know how to handle ourselves."

Finn nodded and jerked his thumb at the dojo. "Show me what you've got."

"Sir?" Ronan's brow crinkled. "You want us to spar with each other?"

Finn chuckled. "I want you to spar with me." He drained the coffee cup, handed it to Mila, and motioned for them to follow.

The twins glanced at one another again, then shrugged. "Okay," they said in unison.

---

Finn wiped perspiration from his forehead and tossed the towel onto a weapons rack. "Not bad. You two are more advanced than I thought."

The twins were lying on the mat, sucking deep breaths and drenched in sweat. Ronan gave a weak thumbs-up without looking his way.

Finn chuckled and grabbed a couple of waters from their stocked mini-fridge. He walked over, handed the bottles and a fresh towel to each selkie, and sat cross-legged on the mat nearby.

The twins both slowly sat up and twisted off the caps to chug half the water down.

Finn gazed at them. "This mission could go one of two ways. Either it will be a walk in the park and you'll be in no danger whatsoever, or we could start a war and have to fight our way out. Are you two good with that?"

They both nodded, and Regan wiped sweat from her face before answering, "We talked things over with Kevin last night. The Dark Star can't be allowed to use a ship like the *Anthem*. It would mean a world war, even if it was so the Peabrains could get their hands on the ship. If the stories about her are true, the Dark Star will kill millions to reach her goals."

Ronan nodded. "What she wants to accomplish isn't all that bad, if you ask me. A place where magicals can be themselves and get the help from a government that knows they exist would be fantastic, but not at the cost she's planning to exact. There has to be another way."

Ronan's answer surprised Finn. It showed a level of thought he didn't associate with young people. Maybe it was because they had been raised one step from the streets, relying on their clan.

"It's more than avoiding war," Mila said as she entered the dojo with two towels draped over her arm. "If the Dark Star uses the ship, there is no way to keep magic hidden any longer. That knowledge alone would start all kinds of trouble. People would start hunting magicals in the streets. Hell, we do that to our own kind for much less than magical abilities."

She handed a clean towel to each. "There are showers in

the locker room. You two need to clean up after that display."

Ronan shrugged. "We're close to home, and we have the car. We should get back and pack for the trip."

"Sounds like a plan," Finn said, rising to his feet and offering a hand to help the twins up. They both stood up and took another long pull of water.

Regan cleared her throat. "Um, would it be okay for us to bring our Playstation? I mean, it sounds like we might have some downtime, and I'm guessing Preston Meriwether's TV at the cabin will be the shit."

Finn shrugged, not knowing what a Playstation was. "Have at it."

They lit up with wide grins and high-fived one another. "Sweet! Okay, we'll get things together and meet you here in the morning."

"Be careful driving home," Mila cautioned, folding the clean towels back up. "It's been snowing ever since you got here."

Regan smiled. "No problem. We were born and raised here. Snow is a way of life. Besides, knowing Denver weather, it'll melt in ten minutes anyway."

Mila chuckled. "True."

The twins bundled up in their puffy jackets, pulled on matching knit caps at the door, made their goodbyes, and headed out.

As soon as Mila closed the door behind them, a huffing Danica pushed it open again. Her face red from exertion, she gulped a few breaths.

Mila stepped back to let the puffing elf in. "Hey, babe.

Did you just run a marathon? I don't think I've ever seen you so out of breath."

Danica dropped a plastic bag from the corner store on the counter, shrugged out of her coat and scarf, and tossed them on the bench under the coat rack beside the door.

"I think it was one of those stupid hitmen the Dark Star sent after you guys." She leaned straight-armed against the counter.

"What?" Mila's eyes widened. She stepped over and rubbed a comforting hand on Danica's back. "How do they even know about you?"

"Well, we do all live together," Finn said, cocking his head and glancing around the condo with a sudden spike of fear. "Where's Penny?"

Danica waved off his worry as she took a deep breath. "Outside working on the wards. She saw me coming and scared off the two guys following me. Blew a stream of fire at them. They jumped into a van and sped off."

Finn and Mila exchanged a look. "Was it a black cargo van?"

Danica nodded. She chuckled and pulled a bottle of white wine and a couple of bags of chips out of the bag.

"I'll check the listing on the phone," Mila said, jogging toward her room.

"Maybe you should take a few days off until we settle this with the Dark Star," Finn said, worry thick in his voice. "I wouldn't know what to do if you got hurt because of all this."

She gave him a halfhearted smile. "That's sweet, Finn, but I don't want to be cooped up in here because I'm too afraid to go outside. That's no way to live. Besides, I can take care of myself. I just need to be more prepared."

"That fucking whore!" Mila shouted, coming out of her room with the assassin's phone in her hand. "She put a bounty on Danica too. A million dollars, dead. Not dead or alive, just dead." Mila slammed the phone down.

Danica's eyes went wide, and she gulped. "She wants me dead? Why?"

"She's trying to get to us. She knows we have access to the bounty board," Finn growled. He glanced at Danica, who appeared more fearful now that it was right in front of her. "Screw it. Take the next week off. You're coming with us. You can stay at the cabin, which is warded better than this place. And, if we need it, you can patch us up after we tear her men to pieces while we check out the ship. This is personal now. No one fucks with my friends."

## CHAPTER NINE

F inn handed a metal keycard to Danica. "Preston's cabin. Keep this, so there aren't any problems when you get there."

Danica hung up the phone after having called in sick for the next week. She took the card and a flash of light nearly blinded them all.

"Oh, shit! I forgot about that!" Danica blinked a few times. "Okay, aren't you guys coming with me?"

Finn shook his head. "I'll see if Hermin can teleport you and the selkie twins there tomorrow morning. Me and Mila need to drive. We don't know how much travel we'll have to do once we're there, so having a vehicle will make it easier."

Mila nodded. "Plus, once this is all over, we can go to the hot springs down the road. A nice long soak will make this all worth it."

Danica gave her a sidelong glance. "Maybe not worth it, but it'll help."

"I don't know," Mila teased. "They're *really* nice."

The French door to the balcony opened and Finn spun. He relaxed when he observed Penny coming inside, her wards evidently finished.

"Any problems?" he asked.

Penny flapped over to them, shaking her head. "Shi chi shir."

"Good. That should keep the place safe while we're gone. Did you get a good look at the men who were after Danica?"

Penny nodded. "Chi chi. Shir shee squee." She waved a hand, saying they were harmless buffoons.

Finn laughed. The two women looked at her inquisitively. "She said she chased the buffoons into the river at the 15th Street bridge. Cops arrived on the scene before they got to shore."

"That's lucky," Mila said, fist-bumping Penny after she landed on Finn's shoulder.

"You two pack. I have an errand; be back in a couple hours," Finn said, walking over to the coatrack. He pulled his Frankenstein bomber jacket on.

"Where are you going?" Mila raised an eyebrow. "Is it a good idea, with all these assholes running around out there?"

"Eh, with Penny chasing the last ones into the river, they'll be taking it easy while they regroup. Anyway, I have Fragar and the temper to match. I'm going to pick up a few things from the market. Coming with me, Penny?"

Penny landed on his shoulder, blowing a smoke ring from her nostril.

He narrowed his eyes at her. "You want to get some of those tooters from the street meat cart, don't you?"

Penny shrugged, but her stomach grumbled loud enough for them all to hear.

Finn chuckled. "Okay, a tooter sounds good, to tell the truth. Hey, Danica?"

She looked up from her phone. "Yeah?"

"Pack your bow. Just in case."

She sharply nodded. "Already planned on it."

"Good. See you two in a bit." He stepped into the hall and closed the door behind him.

While he was riding the elevator down, Finn considered what Ronan had said about how the Dark Star might have the wrong execution, but her intentions weren't all that far off. It had plagued Finn's thoughts ever since he'd first heard about the woman. He and Penny had been all over the universe and seen oodles of cultures, but if one thing was a constant, an oppressed or hidden section of a society would eventually boil over.

"Chi?" Penny scratched at his hair, leaning forward to peek at him.

"Huh? Oh, nothing. Thinking about where this is all leading," Finn said as the elevator dinged. He stepped into the small lobby and went through the glass door to the street. A gust of air worked its way through his open jacket, making him zip it up. Cold never bothered him, but he got fewer strange looks when he acted like a Peabrain. Not that having a blue-winged lizard on his shoulder didn't draw its fair share of looks, but the people in LoDo were used to seeing the odd pet or two. The district was a hipster mecca.

He passed through inch-deep fresh snow on top of

packed snow from earlier foot traffic. The stuff had kept falling since that morning, and it coated the city in a few inches of white powder that was not yet gray and slushy. The fluffy snow gave the city an otherworldly feel, muting the usual sounds and making the world small and lonely.

Finn peered at the pinprick of sun fighting to be seen through the gray sky. He judged it was around lunchtime, so he made haste before the lunch crowd filled the streets. Their manic hour of eating and errands fascinated him as he watched from the condo's balcony. They flooded the streets with cars and the sidewalks with people in business suits, stuffing food in their mouths or making deposits at banks before disappearing again—sudden raiding parties pillaging at prescribed hours.

Finn hurried across the street in case someone didn't understand how traction and snow worked. His thoughts returned to how lunch hour was a very Peabrain idea, which led him to how most magicals were not represented in society, and how that was a pressure cooker with a clogged relief valve. Something must give.

"Chi shir?" Penny piped up again, hunkering against his neck to keep the wind at bay.

"I was thinking about what this world will look like in a few decades," he told her, deciding that talking things out might lead him to an understanding. "Ronan wasn't the first to suggest the Dark Star's intentions are good even if not needed. For now, at least, most people can see her methods are insane, but that won't always be true. That magicals aren't even being oppressed compounds the issue. It's like they all made a deal with one another, except now they're starting to see it was a bad one."

Penny gathered her thoughts as Finn turned down the alley behind the bodega. Once they entered the tight alley and the wind died, Penny sat up, shaking out her wings before settling down again. "Shi, chi chi?" she asked, coming up empty.

Finn shrugged, making her take a handful of his hair to keep her balance. "I don't know what to do either. I mean, is there anything I *can* do? I feel like if there was something that could be done, Preston and his people would have thought of it already."

"Suqee shir. Chi shee."

"They're still magicals," Finn argued, pounding on the brick wall where the Market's entrance was. "You think they're, what, too close to the problem to see the solution?"

A brick slid back, and a pair of large feline eyes took them in. "Password?"

"Peabrains are forgetful," Finn said. "How's it going, Pete?"

"Can't complain. Welcome back." The brick slid back in place and an arch of bubbles formed around the entrance.

"Chi shee shee," Penny continued as the door formed.

Finn thought about that, not replying until they were halfway down the hundred steps to the Market. "That's interesting. They grew up like this. Most of them don't even remember what it means to live in a normal society. That brings up whether we *should* do anything about it. Isn't this how societies evolve? Who are we to impose our beliefs on them?"

Penny shrugged but lost interest as soon as the sweet, meaty smell of tooters hit her snout. She made a grabbing motion. Finn chuckled, pulled a few dollars out of his back pocket, and slapped them into her outstretched hand. "Make sure to get me one this time."

Penny nodded and followed her nose down the stairs, leaving Finn to take the last fifty steps by himself. He could swear he saw several drops of drool in her wake.

# CHAPTER TEN

The Market's whitewashed brick and stone walls and vaulted ceiling brought a lightness to the underground chamber that made the thin haze of smoke and incense less noticeable. The lanterns on the walls and hanging from the arched ceiling beams emitted some light, but most came from magical means that illuminated the air, giving mundane objects an otherworldly cast.

Finn stepped into the flow of foot traffic along the first row of stalls. A pair of elves, their heads close together as they spoke and examined an object in their hands, nearly ran into him, sidestepping at the last second. They gave him dark looks until they saw who he was, then glanced away, picking up their pace.

Finn frowned. People were talking about him, and the old prejudices were ingrained deep. He shrugged. He couldn't blame them for thinking ill of dwarves. It was a well-earned reaction, considering the heavy hand his ancestors had used to rule them.

Finn fell into step with the crowd, not in any hurry and

not knowing where to find what he sought. He visited a few booths with magical items, but they were barely worth a second look—mere spell charms and ritual components.

Most races used the same process to cast spells: create a bubble, change reality inside it, and then release the bubble to introduce the magic into reality. Finn's teachers had explained the details when he was young, but he didn't remember most of his lessons since he was always struggling with his rage. The takeaway was that magic was easier for most than for dwarves. The way he saw it, the power of a caster's will determined their strengths: larger will, larger spell. Most folks lacked the will—and imagination—to use their powers to the fullest extent, so they relied on rituals or components, and those were what filled most of the booths.

"See anything you like, my lord?"

Finn discerned a young man with shaggy black hair that hung around his face, hiding it. Finn couldn't determine his race, although pointed ears poked out of his black mop. The youth wrung his hands, a hint of worry in his posture.

Finn displayed his white teeth through his thick brown beard. "Sorry. You don't carry what I need."

"What is it you seek? I know most of the vendors here. Perhaps I can point you in the right direction?"

His willingness to help took Finn by surprise, considering it was obvious he was nervous about having the infamous dwarf at his stall. It dawned on Finn that he was the only one *at* the stall. Passersby avoided the booth soon as they saw him. The young man was trying to move him along.

Finn was willing to do so. The problem was he didn't know how to ask for what he wanted. It wasn't illegal, but he found most magicals frowned upon their use, at least here on Earth. He was about to tell the young man to forget it and amble on when he remembered the elven leader from the warped trees incident. He had told him where he had gotten the dwarven amulet.

"Actually…" Finn leaned in, resting a hand on the table, "do you know where I can find a Tommy?"

The man narrowed his eyes in thought. "A Tommy? What's that?"

Finn shook his head. " Not a what, a who."

Leaning back and breathing out an "oh," he nodded. "I think you mean 'Timmy.'"

Finn snapped his fingers. "Right. Sorry, Timmy. Do you know where I can find him?"

He pointed to the far corner of the Market. "Large green tent that way, up against the wall. The sign over the door says Whatever."

Finn furrowed his brow. "Whatever, as in 'I don't care?'"

The man laughed and his hair came apart enough that Finn spied a hooked nose, its tip as black and shiny as obsidian.

"Whatever, as in he has whatever you need," he said, the corner of his mouth up in a half-smile.

Finn scanned the table before him and found a small metal charm that was an accurate representation of Fragar on a looped bit of string. He picked it up and examined it. "What is this for?" Finn didn't detect any magic.

"You put it on your phone or keys or whatever."

He let the charm hang by the string and held it close to

his face, taking in the details. "Does it let you locate the object it's attached to?"

The young man's head and hair shook. "No, man. It's just an ornament. It doesn't do anything except look cool."

"Oh." Finn pulled a roll of cash from his pocket. "How much?"

The guy eyeballed the roll of bills, licking his lips before letting his shoulders sag—a sign he'd considered a swindle, then given up on the idea. Finn was glad to see it. He liked the black-haired moptop.

"Twenty bucks?"

Finn handed him a fifty and put the charm in his pocket. "Keep it. Thanks for pointing me the right way."

The guy goggled at the fifty, then reached out, stopping Finn before he could step away. "Hey, sorry about earlier. I was trying to get you out of here. I don't know if you know this or not, but people in the community are wary of you. We all grew up with tales of dwarves, and they're not what you'd call flattering. Hell, the last dwarves on Earth were the Vikings, and we all know they were a bunch of assholes." He shook his head, waving away the comment. "Point is, people who've met you are saying you're a good dude. I didn't believe them, but..." He held up the fifty and shook it. "Turns out you're an okay sort."

Finn held out a hand. The young man looked at it and extended his, and they pumped hands in a solid shake. "Thanks. I wouldn't mind if you spread the word." Finn smiled, letting go and thumbing the straps of his harness like a farmer surveying his fields.

"I will. And, hey, a heads up. Timmy can be shady sometimes on prices. Don't flash your wad until you agree on a price."

Finn held back a laugh, considering the young man had almost done that very thing to him. "I'll keep my wits about me. What's your name?"

"Holbrook," he said, taking a step back and sitting on a stool next to the table that held his wares.

"Holbrook. I'll remember that." Finn tipped an imaginary hat to him. "See you around, kid."

After making his way to the back of the Market, he found the large green tent. It took up the space of four stalls, spread out against the whitewashed wall. The entrance was pinned open, and warm yellow light filtered out into the path.

Finn stepped in and the sounds of the market disappeared, replaced by the crackle of flame and smell of incense in the air. A double row of tall shelves kept him from seeing beyond the wares on display. An aisle split the rows, allowing a view of green cloth at the back of the tent, where lined tables exhibited more items. Hanging braziers with low flames hung from the central beam.

Finn proceeded down the center aisle, checking the rows to be sure there wasn't anyone else in the tent. He wondered if he was feeling the effects of a dampening spell. When he got to the back wall, he checked both ways, not seeing anyone, but spying a counter tucked into the far right corner. Nobody occupied it, but he saw a crystal formation behind it that made him do a double-take.

As he headed down the row, Finn marveled at the crystal. It had to weigh several tons and was clear as glass. He noted cut edges, so it had been formed to a degree, but along the top and back ridges, spikes stuck out anywhere from an inch to a foot. He couldn't determine its composition, but he guessed it could be a pure diamond. Priceless, even in these far reaches of the universe.

Finn leaned over the wooden countertop for a better look and jumped back when the crystal structure sat up and regarded him with emerald eyes.

"Can I help you?" the diamond asked, its voice high and childlike.

Finn's mouth open and closed a few times, unable to put together a sentence.

The diamond blinked, then frowned. "Haven't you seen a crystal golem before?"

"Uh, yeah, but not one made of diamond!"

The giant was hard to read because he was prismatic and slowly changed expressions, as if he operated at half speed compared to the world around him.

His mouth split into a glacier-slow smile, showing off perfectly formed diamond teeth. "You like it? I grew it myself." He lifted a foot-thick arm, admiring it in the firelight.

The childlike voice threw the interaction off for Finn. He had expected a deep and rumbling voice, like the golems he'd come across. He wondered if the diamond body had something to do with it. Perhaps it vibrated at a higher frequency or something.

Finn recovered and approached the counter, noting the creature's size. "I'm looking for Timmy. That wouldn't be you, would it?"

A slow nod sent light dancing across the tent's ceiling. "At your service, dwarf. Finnegan, is it?"

"How did you know that?"

Timmy shrugged. "People talk. I like to listen. Never know when it might be worth something."

Finn had dealt with info brokers almost as often as store owners. If it was valuable, they'd find a way to profit, and rarely did favors come from them without one in return.

"I hear you deal some in dwarven artifacts?" Finn, now composed, grinned and leaned an elbow on the counter. "Don't suppose you would mind showing me what you have? The good stuff. I don't have use for charms and trinkets, if you know what I mean."

Timmy nodded, then gazed at the ceiling in thought. It seemed some body language was universal. "I don't have anything in stock at the moment, but you might convince me to let you know what comes in...for a finder's fee."

Finn snorted. "How much are we talking?"

"Five hundred upfront."

"To let me know when you get something in? That's outrageous." Finn had the money, but he knew if he agreed right away, he would be overcharged for everything he tried to buy here for the rest of his life.

"If you wish to pass, no diamond dust off my back." He made to turn away.

"How about this?" Finn put a hand on Timmy's arm. The diamond was freezing cold and made his fingers numb. He snatched his hand back and blew on his fingers.

"You have a counteroffer?" Timmy prompted.

Sticking his hand in his pocket, Finn said, "I'll give you five hundred, but it goes toward the purchase price of the artifact if I buy it. If I don't, you can keep it."

"That works for me," Timmy agreed. He pulled on a giant rubber glove and extended his large hand. Finn tried to shake it, but Timmy's hand was so big he ended up gripping his pointer finger and shaking it like a child.

Finn knew Timmy would simply raise the price by five hundred when he came in, but it made him look less like a pushover. He turned, pulled out his roll of bills, peeled five hundreds off the stack, and stuffed the rest back into his pocket. He turned back and handed the bills to the giant, who plucked them from him.

"Will that be all?" Timmy asked, a smile on his clear face.

"I'm looking for something that's hard to find. I hear you're the man, or golem in this case, to talk to." Finn leaned a hip on the counter, letting the tension build. "I need a rifle."

Timmy blinked twice. "There are gun stores on every street corner up there." He pointed a thick finger at the ceiling. "Go see a Peabrain about that."

"I need a magical one—something that doesn't make a lot of noise, but has a good amount of power." He described the rifle Preston had loaned Mila during the hunt for the hellhounds.

Timmy listened, nodding along until Finn finished. "I know the type you're looking for."

"Great." Finn rubbed his hands together. "How much will it cost me?"

"Oh, I don't have one. I do know what you're talking about however."

Finn's face fell. "Oh. Well, shit. I guess I can add that to the list of things to tell me about when they come in." He pulled out one of the cards Penny had made up with his name and number on it and slid it across the counter.

He turned to go.

"I *do* have a pistol if that would work," the childlike voice continued.

# CHAPTER ELEVEN

M ila sat on the edge of Danica's king-sized bed, her feet not touching the floor as she leaned back on outstretched arms and crossed her ankles. She watched as Danica went through her dresser picking out clothes she wanted to take to the cabin.

Danica turned and held up a sky blue bikini top with white polka dots to her chest. "What do you think about this one?"

"Super cute. Goes with your pale skin like it was made for you," Mila said, not knowing what to say. "Um, you seem to be taking this whole having a bounty on your head pretty well."

Danica shrugged, pulling out the matching bottoms to the bikini. She stuffed them in her duffel before pulling out a second swimsuit, a monokini with more fabric than the previous top alone. She held the shiny black swimsuit up, turning one way then the other, looking down at herself before tossing it back in the drawer.

"I guess I kind of expected it," Danica said, rooting

deeper into the drawer. She extracted a basic black bikini. She didn't even ask about that one, just stuffed it into her duffel and kept looking. "The moment I met Finn I knew my life would be harder, but I also knew it would be better."

Mila laughed. "How is fighting off hitmen and assassins better?"

"Well, it's exciting." She turned and held up a burnt orange top with black edges and straps. "You like this one?"

"Yeah. I like that a lot."

Danica threw it to Mila along with the bottoms. "Good. I can't get away with orange, it makes my skin look too pink, and it goes better with your complexion. I think I bought it when we first met. God, I wanted to be tan back then." She chuckled, and moved to the next drawer, hesitated, reached into the first drawer, and stuffed the monokini into her duffel. She gave Mila a coy smile. "Maybe Phil can come up when this is all over."

"Oh, yeah. The morgue guy." Mila crossed her legs and tucked her bare feet under her. "How's that going? Why don't you ever bring him over? I feel you're having a secret love affair behind my back."

Danica pulled out several pairs of panties Mila thought had too much lace for a dangerous mission. Then again, she wasn't sure Danica owned any other kind.

"Well, I can't bring him here, what with Penny doing Penny things and us having a full blown dojo in the living room. He's not 'in the know,' as it were. I think he's self conscious to be seen with me." She folded the underwear and placed them in the duffel before putting her hands on her hips and scrutinizing her selections. "How long do you think we'll be up there?"

Mila tucked her hair behind her ear, leaned forward, and rested her elbows on her knees. "I don't know. Preston said the keys will work for a month. If we need longer, he can extend them. I don't see why we would need to be there that long. I feel like this is all going to come crashing down soon." Mila stared into the distance, trying to envision how it would all end and coming up blank. "Didn't you only take off a week?"

"Yeah, but I have an insane amount of vacation days. I've never missed a day at the hospital and the vacation rolls over forever. I could take the next six months off if I wanted, although I wouldn't want to do that to my patients." She considered for a few seconds, then pulled out a second stack of underwear and put them in the bag beside the first stack. "Eh, better safe than naked."

Mila laughed. "Not something I thought to hear you say. You like to be naked a lot. I'm surprised you don't still make your naked trips to the laundry every other day."

"I can't do that! At least not when Finn's here. I check before I come out now, but you're usually with Finn, so you don't get the show anymore," she said with fake haughtiness before pulling out a stack of thick fleece leggings and packing them. "I think that's about it. Bathroom stuff in there, clothes for two weeks in here, bathing suits for the hot springs, and that bag has my shoes." She pointed to a second duffel bulging with footwear.

"You brought outdoor gear, right? Hiking boots, thermal underwear, and what not?"

Danica imparted her a sarcastic glare. "I may be blonde,

but I dye my hair, thank you very much. Come on, we need to get you and Finn packed."

Mila scooted off the bed. She followed Danica into the living room and toward her room. "I have to say, I have known a lot of dumb people, but I can't say they were mostly blonde. Where did that idea even come from?"

"The eighties," Danica said, opening the door to Mila's room and heading straight for her closet.

Mila glanced over and saw the large female orb weaver spider cradled in her web beside the window. "You doing all right? Not getting too hungry?"

She had opened the window a crack and blocked all but a small hole for the spider to come and go as she pleased. The yellow and black orb weaver bowed, and Mila's mind filled with an affirmative and appreciative feeling.

"Good. We'll be gone a while, so you'll have the place to yourself. Try not to cover the whole house in webs." She chuckled at the shocked feeling coming from the spider at such an admonishment. She asserted she couldn't make that much web if her life depended on it; not in winter, at least, when food was so scarce.

"What did you say?" Danica came out of the walk-in, her arm draped with dresses.

"Nothing." Mila looked at the dresses and frowned. "Why did you bring those out?"

Danica started laying them on the made bed. "So you can pick one to take." She laid five dresses out and returned to the closet.

"I don't need a dress. If you remember, this is a mission to find the *Anthem* and disable it if we can. When am I going to have time to wear something like this?"

Danica returned with five sets of shoes and placed them with the dress she thought best accompanied them. She stepped back and put her hands on her hips to survey the matches. She switched the shoes on two dresses.

She turned to Mila. "This is for your date. Now, choose."

"What date?" Mila turned red.

"With Finn."

Mila felt the heat on her cheeks and hated the betrayal. "I don't have a date with Finn. We aren't dating. That's not a thing."

Danica put her hands on Mila's shoulders and looked her in the eyes. "It *is* a thing. I know it. Penny knows it. Hell, even you know it. Finn doesn't seem to know it, but we can fix that. You deserve to be happy. I remember the douche canoes you used to date, back when you still had time for dating and you weren't some museum bigshot. Finn is a good man."

"Actually, he's a dwarf."

"I think the PC term is 'little people,' sweetie."

They stared at one another for a beat before they cracked up. Mila wrapped her arms around Danica's waist and hugged her. "I miss the two of us hanging out," she said, pressing her cheek against Danica's chest.

"Me too." Danica kissed the top of her head, then pushed Mila to arms' length. "But I like how it is now with Finn and Penny too. Those two are good for us. Without them, you wouldn't know I'm an elf, and we would have kept going to our jobs and grown old together. I love you, and I don't want to be the two old ladies who people talk about. I want to be alive and have adventures and, you know, save the world. We have a great life, assassins and all, and I want us to have an even better one. Which is why you're going on a date with a prince." She spun Mila around to face the bed. "Now, choose one."

"Okay, Mom."

Danica slapped her on the ass hard enough to make Mila jump and grab her butt cheek. "Atta boy!" She laughed and skipped to Mila's dresser. "That was for the other night. I don't think you know your own strength when you get a few beers in you."

Mila rubbed at her stinging butt cheek as she looked the dresses over. Three of them were black, one was red, and the last was a green one she had bought but never worn. "I have a lot of black clothes."

Danica didn't look up from the drawer she was rooting through. "Black looks good on you. I mean, it looks good on everyone, but especially on you."

Mila sighed. She would have to fold all those clothes again. "Well, you picked open-toed shoes for these two, so they're out."

"You have cute toes! Why throw out the dress just because of the shoes?"

"One word. Snow. And I don't want to lose these cute toes to frostbite." She scanned the selections and pointed at the red dress. "This. The red one."

Danica turned. "It's because I chose boots for that one, isn't it?"

"Yup." Mila picked up the other four and headed toward the closet.

"How do you not have any sexy underwear?" Danica yanked a second drawer open. She rummaged around and froze. She pulled out a pair and stared before turning to face Mila and hold the offending underwear in front of her. They were a bright yellow bikini brief with a Pikachu face on the crotch.

"Are you serious?" Danica sounded like she had been stabbed in the back.

Mila laughed. "Remember Roy?"

"The lazy slob who spilled chocolate milk on our couch? Yeah. I remember."

"He was into Pokémon. I got those as a gift after he went to the Denver Comic-Con. He thought they were sexy."

"Holy shit. Your previous choices in men makes me wonder about you." Danica tossed the briefs into the drawer and pulled out the most impractical lacy G-string ever made and held it up. "It's like nothing in between. Why do you even have this? It's like wearing floss that saws at your asshole all day."

"Another gift. I put them on for all of ten minutes to show him, then stuffed them in a drawer."

"Why didn't you throw them away? Or use them to strangle the guy who bought them?" She tossed them in the wastebasket beside the nightstand.

"I like to keep it simple, I guess." Mila shrugged, putting the shoes in their proper places in the closet.

"You got that right. All I can see in here are cotton bikini briefs and boyshorts. How can you be so fashionable when we go out and so plain underneath? I don't even see any cheekys in here."

Mila furrowed her brow. "What are cheekys?"

Danica turned, eyes wide. "Are you serious? Right.

That's it." She held her hand up, and the room filled with the scent of winter in a deep forest. A bubble formed in her palm.

Mila stared in fascination. She had seen Danica do magic before, but only when saving lives, not in their everyday life. She figured Danica was used to holding back since she lived most of her life with a Peabrain that didn't know magic existed. Mila felt sorry that she had stifled her friend all those years, even if she didn't know she'd done it.

The bubble popped. Danica smiled and marched into the living room. "Put some shoes and socks on. We're going out."

"We can't just leave. Assassins out there, remember?" Still, she grabbed a pair of socks and followed Danica.

"Don't worry. No one will see us. I arranged a ride." She slipped into a pair of kneehigh boots.

"What ri—" Mila jumped back and yelped.

A six foot tall bubble materialized in the center of the living room and popped in her face. Hermin stood there, his hands in a fighting pose as he glanced around the room. "Where are they?"

"Where are who?" Danica zipped her second boot up and stood from the arm of the couch.

"You said it was an emergency." He deflated, his cheeks red from adrenaline.

"It is. We need to go to the mall."

Hermin stared, struggling to see if she were joking, and then let out a snort. "You know, I'm busy, right? This ship needs a lot of attention. I don't have time for random shopping trips. What in the four engines could you need so badly it can't wait?"

"Sexy underwear, Hermin. Lots of sexy underwear." She put a hand on his shoulder and squeezed. "You can help us pick them out."

Hermin's eyes glazed over. "Break time anyway. Let's go."

CHAPTER TWELVE

Finn ducked under the cloth entry of Whatever and stepped into the bustling Market. After the hour he had spent haggling in the magically silenced tent, the Market's clamor hit him like a hammer.

Finn figured Timmy would drive a hard bargain for the pistol, but he never imagined how hard. The ten grand he'd had in cash still wasn't enough. In the end, the magical pistol had cost him all the cash he had on him with the added promise of an introduction to Preston Meriwether.

Finn called Preston to explain. At first, the man refused. When he learned the pistol was for Mila, he changed his mind, but *only* if Finn updated him on how things played out when she used it. Finn didn't understand that until Preston explained the pistol didn't use bullets. It used raw magic for its projectiles. Finn started to reconsider. He didn't detect magic from Mila. If she was recovering, it might do more harm than good. Finn grilled Timmy on the gun's properties after that, and he learned it used a tiny bit of magic, although it never pulled more than was available. In the end, he decided it might be a good measure of her abilities without the danger of overtaxing her.

They struck a deal, and Finn handed over his cash and gave Timmy the number Preston provided. They shook hands again—or, in Finn's case, shook finger—and Timmy packed the gun into a fancy wooden case made specifically for it.

Finn glanced down the aisles, wondering where Penny had gotten off to, but decided she was a big girl. Knowing her, she was passed out from stuffing her face.

The ornate gun case under his arm had one more stop to make. He made his way through the Market until he came to a drab brown tent with no signage. Finn ducked inside. The smell of cured leather and polish filled his nostrils as he adjusted to the dim lighting from a couple of old-fashioned lanterns suspended from the ceiling.

The shop was small, with a middle divider separating the workshop from the sales floor. Racks lined the walls and displayed various leather items, everything from clothing to armor in sizes from tiny to massive.

Finn fingered a few exceptional pieces on his way to the counter. He set the case down and rang a little bell beside a stack of notebooks. One of the books was open. Finn appreciated the detailed sketch of a leather skirt with sheaths for throwing knives built into the pleats.

"You like that?" An older Peabrain with a white topknot and a trimmed white beard stepped from the back, wiping leather polish from his hands with a stained rag. "Thought it up after watching *Smoking Aces 2*. Martha Higareda always ended up stripping to get to her weapons. I thought this was a more elegant solution than fighting in a leather teddy." He cocked his head. "Not as sexy, but practical."

Finn extended his hand and offered a big smile. "Joseph. How are you?"

The leatherworker's grip was firm and strong from years of detail work. "Doing great, Finn. How did that belt turn out for your girlfriend?"

Finn chuckled. "Perfect. That's why I came here. I need to make an addition to it. Oh, and she's not my girlfriend."

Joseph narrowed his eyes. "Mm-hm. Whatever you say. Though you could have fooled me the way you went on about her. Okay, so what do you want to add?"

Finn let it go. He turned the case toward Joseph and opened it.

The man leaned to inspect the weapon, then glanced up and motioned at it. "Do you mind?"

"Not at all. You'll need to handle it to make the holster." Finn slid the case toward him.

Joseph pulled the pistol out, turning it over in his hands and examining the weapon's lines. It wasn't a large gun, six inches from the tip of the barrel to the end of the weapon, but it looked even smaller in Joseph's thick fingers.

"Where the hell did you get this?" he asked, before putting it back in the case.

"Timmy at Whatever. Paid a pretty penny for it."

"I bet. This is an Ivar. Extremely rare. One of the few artifacts elves and dwarves made together. The thing is practically indestructible, and it never runs out of ammo. Shit, man, did you sell your soul for this?" He fetched one of his notebooks and opened it to a clean page, then he grabbed a piece of charcoal and began sketching.

"No, nothing like that. He did charge ten grand though."

Joseph's head snapped up. "That's it? Ten grand? There had to be something else."

"He wanted a meeting with Preston Meriwether. That's it." Because of Joseph's reaction, Finn felt worried. Why had Timmy let it go for so little?

Joseph narrowed his eyes and did the math in his head. "Either he didn't know what he had, which I doubt, or he has something up his sleeve. Maybe he sees it as an investment."

"Could Preston be in danger?"

Joseph laughed and returned to sketching. "Hell, no. One thing we can count on, that diamond bastard will never slaughter his golden geese. He knows the long game. It comes from being practically immortal. No, if he gets in good with Preston, he'll ride that train forever and cash in at every stop." He made a few more lines on the page, and Finn noticed he had completed the rough. Joseph stared at it for a few seconds, then glanced at Finn. "This should take thirty minutes or so if you want to wait, or you could grab a bite."

"I need to find Penny before she eats herself to death. I'll stop back in half an hour. Oh, shit..." Finn's face reddened with embarrassment. "I gave all my money to Timmy!"

Joseph waved him off. "I know you're good for it. You can bring it next time."

"Thanks. Sorry about that."

"Hey, count yourself lucky all you got taken for was

your money. Like they said in *Tommy Boy*; that guy can sell a ketchup popsicle to a woman in white gloves."

"Ketchup popsicle?"

"Yeah! You've seen the movie?"

Finn shook his head. He had no clue what Joseph was on about. He filed *Tommy Boy* away for later viewing. "I'll catch you in a bit. Thanks."

Ten minutes later, Finn found Penny in a paper hotdog boat at Gwen the Dryad's food cart. The tiny woman and dragon were laughing and drawing the attention of everyone around, mostly because Gwen's piercing laugh cut through the Market's commotion, and gouts of flame accompanied Penny's laughter.

Finn wove around various picnic tables and diners and arrived to hear Gwen tell the end of a filthy joke. Penny clutched her stomach and howled with laugher, shooting geysers of flame into the air.

"Good fortune to you and your saplings, Gwen," Finn said, using the formal greeting for a dryad. He liked the spunky old Fey, and courtesy went a long way with her kind.

"Still a charmer, I see. Princes are at least taught good manners." Gwen displayed a sharp-toothed smile and batted her large eyes. "You'll be wantin' one of my tooters, I suppose? Penny's ate four already."

"I would love one, but I got cleaned out at the last booth, I'm afraid."

She opened the fifty-five gallon drum while giving him a narrow-eyed stare. "You paid enough last time. I can spare you a freebie." She whipped a large pair of tongs from a hook built onto the grill, clacked them, and picked out a good tooter. She plucked the blue larvae off the hot surface and dropped it into a paper boat, then selected a second one and put it in another boat. She handed Finn the first boat and the bubbling glaze over the three-inch larvae let off little clouds of steam. Gwen slid the second tooter to Penny, who cheered before digging in, ignoring the heat.

"She's been keepin' me entertained. That's worth a fuckin' tooter, I reckon." She picked some gristle from between her teeth and sucked air through them. "What else can I do for you?"

"I was looking for Penny. It's a bonus she led me here to you."

She clacked the tongs in his face, and he flinched. "Don't give me that line of bullshit. Your charms are useless against me, dwarf. Well, mostly useless."

She came out around her grill and hopped onto one of the picnic table benches. Finn joined her, setting his tooter down to cool.

"Penny tells me there's a woman in your life. This the same gal you had that favor made for?"

Gwen referred to their first meeting. At the time, he had sought someone who could make him a gift for Mila to thank her for her help when he'd first arrived on Earth. The favor was not only his promise to her but a magical artifact obligating him to undertake any favor she asked. By giving Mila the rune-inscribed card, Finn was conveying he trusted her judgment and bound himself to her.

"The same. But I wouldn't say she was my 'woman.' Just a friend."

"Okay. Whatever you say, ya dumb shite." She laughed and slapped him on the shoulder.

Finn took a bite of his tooter. The larvae crunched, the sweet meat exploding in his mouth, sending his tastebuds into overdrive. He let out a groan of pleasure. "Iss reary 'ood," he said with his mouth full. A few crumbs shot out, hitting Gwen's apron.

She wiped the bits off with a brush of her hand. "I think Penny eatin' five of the buggers is proof of that. You're goin' to have to carry her out of here. She's eaten her own body weight."

Finn stuffed the rest of the treat into his mouth. He chewed slowly, enjoying the flavors. Gwen watched, her large eyes narrowed.

Finn licked his fingers, not wanting to waste any glaze. He took note of Gwen scrutinizing him. "What? Is some in my beard?" He brushed at his beard, then grabbed his napkin.

"My tree's been talkin' to me," she said, lowering her voice.

Finn raised an eyebrow. "Isn't that...normal?" He tossed the used napkin into the empty paper boat on the table.

She rolled her eyes. "Of course! But what it's sayin', *ain't*." She cleared her throat. "Those fuckin' Huldu don't know their asses from their armpits most the time. Plus, I can't forgive 'em for gettin' us stranded in the middle of nowhere." She bit her tongue to stop her rant and waved her hand to bat the thought away. "Long story short, I didn't know who to tell until you came walkin' around the corner."

Finn leaned his elbow on the table. "Well, I appreciate your faith in my judgment."

She cackled. "I don't have faith in you, dwarf! Not the way you might think. I have experience! Dwarves don't care for things that are out of control. If I have faith in anythin', it's you'll rip some heads off and put this right."

"Thanks?" Finn didn't know if that was a compliment or not. "What is it your tree's been saying?"

Gwen's gaze turned serious. "That the magic around Denver is out of balance."

Finn waited, but it seemed that was it. "What does that mean?"

Gwen put her hands up. "God, you're dense. It means the magic is in flux. There's a power close by that's creatin' or drawin' power and not giving it back."

Finn still didn't get it, but he didn't want to say so and look like a fool.

Gwen was sharp. She saw it on his face and sighed. "Someone is changin' the raw magic to something unusable. Like pollution in the air. If it gets too bad, we won't be able to breathe. Dark magic, ya daft idiot. Someone is using huge amounts of dark magic."

"The Dark Star!" Finn said too loud and peered around. No one showed signs of watching them. He lowered his voice and leaned toward her. "You're saying she's here? In Denver?"

She nodded. "She's close."

"How long has she been here?"

"Not long." She gave him a knowing stare. "Showed up about the same time you did."

"The *Anthem*. It must have notified her the second I

crashed. She stole my ship and hid it, but we know where it is. We're going check it out."

Gwen shook her head. "Maybe it was the ship at first, but she's after you now."

"Why is she after me?"

She slapped him on the back of the head. "Because of this, my prince." She ran a finger over the royal tattoos under his hair. "I hear things from my tree and from those who pass through here. Word is she's gotten her hands on the Gjallarhorn. Now, I know you have no clue what that is, because it was the first thing the dwarves built when we got stuck here. It's an Earth-made object, and trust me when I say it's trouble."

"What is it?" So far, the artifacts Finn had come across were from storage. He hadn't considered things being crafted after the ship got lost.

"Peabrains say it's the horn to announce Ragnarok, but that's religion mixin' with reality. It *is* a horn, true, but it ain't some mystical religious object. It's a distress signal. The dwarves figured if they could make a horn that could be heard across the universe, someone would come for us." She laughed. "In true dwarf fashion, it was ambitious and foolhardy. They made a weapon of unbelievable power. One long note can flatten a forest or destroy an army. Hell, it might be loud enough to hear in the dark expanse, but the power it would take might crack the Earth."

"How do you know all this?"

"I was there when they first used it!" Gwen's gaze turned hazy with memory. "The world shook, and thousands of lives were extinguished in a single note. The dwarves vowed then to find another way to signal for help."

Finn paled. "And she has this Gjallarhorn? Why hasn't she used it?"

Gwen presented a dark smile. "Because the dwarves, while ambitious, are not stupid. The horn can only be used by a dwarf of royal blood." She poked a finger into his chest. "And you're the only royal within a hundred light years."

# CHAPTER THIRTEEN

B y the time he and Penny left the Market, the sun had set. Finn glanced both ways down the alley, lit by sparse lighting. He detected no one and tucked the wooden case under his arm. Joseph had modified the case to hold the gun and also the new black holster. Perfectly formed to fit the gun, the leatherwork even had a spell weaved into it allowing only the wearer of the holster to draw the weapon, keeping it from slipping out or being stolen in a fight. Finn vowed to bring him the money as soon as he could.

During his conversation with Gwen, Penny had laid on her back, holding her distended belly, which made her look pregnant with quadruplets. Dragons processed a lot of food into raw magic, but even Penny's fast digestion couldn't alleviate the discomfort from so many tooters. Only once Finn's errands were finished and they vacated the Market, was she able to move without groaning.

Finn turned down 21st Street and crunched through the falling snow. Penny settled onto his shoulders, draping her neck and body across the back of his neck so her tail was on one shoulder and her head on the other. It wasn't the most comfortable position for Finn, having to keep his head forward to accommodate her, but he didn't protest, knowing she was miserable from tooter gluttony.

The muffled sounds of the city sounded far away. The infrequent vehicle made little noise except for crunching packed snow beneath their tires. It reminded Finn of the winter gardens at his father's palace. The thought of home brought on mixed feelings. A part of him was grateful for the opportunities he'd had, but another part of him resented his parents for forcing him into the army as a berserker, a role he neither wanted or enjoyed.

He didn't leave because he disagreed with his father's politics, or because he found greed for power and money abhorrent—it took him years away to start hating those things. In the end, he left because he no longer wanted to be a killing machine, even if his rage wanted otherwise. Killing was only for certain circumstances. Finn had never shied from it when it was called for, but the way the army encouraged their berserkers to slay indiscriminately sickened him. Stepping away had earned him exile, and he vowed to never return, even if his banishment were lifted.

Ironically, he had still worked for his father in a way. When he came across dangerously powerful dwarven artifacts, he returned them to the family vaults for use at his father's discretion.

Even in exile, he still served the king.

Finn growled, his blood beginning to boil.

"Chi?" Penny stroked his hair, concerned by his burst of emotion.

"I'm fine. Just thinking."

Penny lifted her head as they passed an alley, and she tapped him on the neck, pointing down the shadowy passage.

Finn turned and squinted into the dark. "What is it?"

"Shir," she said, pointing.

He followed her finger and, as his eyes adjusted, spotted something. Against the wall, halfway down the dark alley, Finn made out two Peabrains harassing a smaller figure on the ground clutching what appeared to be a phone.

The sight set Finn's blood boiling again, ramping up from his dark thoughts. He set his jaw and marched into the alley. Penny sensed what was coming and stayed perched on his shoulder, stoking her inner fire and burning off the rest of her meal.

Finn felt her heat on the side of his head, making his ear tingle.

As he got closer, the Peabrain's words carried to him.

"...so fucking weird looking..." One tried to flip their victim's hoodie back, but the small hand shot up and grabbed the edge to keep it down.

"What's the deal, freak? Don't want us seeing yer ugly face?" Both men laughed.

By the way they swayed, Finn could tell they were drunk. He also figured they were around college age, their hoodies displaying the logo of a local university.

"Leave me alone!" The small figure kicked one of them in his shin. He danced back and rubbed at the injury.

Finn felt a flash of fire in his veins. He knew that voice. *Remmy.*

He surged forward, his vision turning red at the edges.

"Fucking bitch!" The uninjured one snatched the front of Remmy's hoodie and pulling back his fist to strike her.

"Shitbags!" Finn roared, mere steps from the one grabbing his shin. Finn balled his fist and cocked his arm back.

The guy stared in a stupefied expression before Finn's fist slammed into his face. He lifted off his feet, flew backward, and landed on his back in the snow.

"My nose!" he screamed, clutching his face as he tried to crab-walk backward.

Something slammed into the side of Finn's head, causing him to stumble sideways a step. He turned to see the second guy, his fists up with an enraged look on his face.

"What's your problem, man?" the guy screamed, taking another swing.

Finn batted the fist away with a swipe of his hand and threw a right jab, hitting the drunk in the chest and knocking the wind out of him. The man went down with a wheeze, clutching his chest.

Penny landed on Remmy's knee, puffed up with dragon's breath in case the fight went badly.

Finn's rage demanded he kill these two. However, the tiny bit of his logical brain told him killing them was wrong. He struggled to calm his bloodlust when the guy with the broken nose charged him and took a clumsy swing at Finn.

Finn saw it coming and bowed his head so the guy's fist hit the hardest part of his skull. The guy screamed, clutching his broken hand.

Finn glared, murder in his eyes. The pair took off

running, stumbling into each other and various trashcans along the way to the street.

Finn fought the instinct to chase them. He watched them turn right and slip on the snow, but they kept their feet and stumbled left out of his line of sight.

He breathed deep, fighting with his rage. A small hand filled his, and he peered down at Remmy looking up from inside her hood. Penny landed on his shoulder and soothed his emotions. The combination of seeing his goblin friend with worry in her eyes and the emotional healing from Penny helped clear his vision.

His breathing calmed, and he knelt to give Remmy a tight smile. "You okay?"

She nodded. "I am now, boss." She had tears in her eyes and threw her arms around his neck. Penny got into the air in time to avoid being crushed between them.

Finn put his arms around Remmy and patted her back. She didn't let up on her hug, and he felt her trembling. "What were you doing out here alone?"

She pulled back, her greenish cheeks wet. She wiped them on her sleeve. "Trying to get some internet. Reception is shit in the sewers." She pulled her beat-up phone out of her pocket.

Something in his core snapped and came free. People suffered over such simple things because they had nowhere to go. Remmy and her tribe were one example. The selkies had to form a gang to meet their needs. Orcs were forced to group together just to be themselves. Something needed to be done.

He gripped Remmy's bony shoulders and smiled. "Why

don't you come to my place? You can use the internet there, and no one will bother you."

"Really?"

"Sure. Maybe we can scrounge up some grub, too."

She hugged him quicker this time but no less fierce. "Thanks, boss!"

They left the alley, and Finn checked the way the two guys had run. To his surprise, Rolf stood at the entrance to the alley. He motioned for Finn to follow with a jerk of his head, then took a long pull from a rolled joint and let the smoke billow up and away into the falling snow.

"Penny, can you take Remmy to the condo?"

Penny glanced at Rolf and shot Finn a questioning glance.

"It's fine. He's a, uh, friend," he said as he stooped to pick up the wooden case and brush the snow off it.

"Shir chi." Penny flapped to land on Remmy's head, her shoulder being too small for the dragon.

Remmy giggled, and Penny pointed in the direction of their condo. Remmy saluted and took off at a skipping run.

Finn watched them until they rounded the corner, then he turned to Rolf. Tucking the wooden case under his arm, he headed toward the old man, wondering what *this* conversation would be like. Judging by the cloud of smoke around Rolf's head, it was going to be either deep or unintelligible. If it meant more enlightenment to help control his rage, Finn was all ears.

# CHAPTER FOURTEEN

F inn slid into the red faux-leather booth inside Gormans 24, a twenty-four hour diner a few blocks from the alley. Rolf flopped down across from him, all smiles and looking baked.

A gray-haired waitress in a pink uniform dress stopped at their booth. "What can I get you?"

Finn peered at her nametag and gave her a polite smile. "Hi, Dottie. I'll take a coffee and a piece of pie."

She started writing on her ticket book. "What kind of pie?"

"I bow to your discretion."

She gave a subtle eyeroll. "Apple it is. You want ice cream?"

"No, thank you."

Dottie turned to Rolf. "You?"

"I'll take the Grand Slam with an extra egg over easy and bacon. A coffee, black, and a large orange juice." He rubbed his hands together in excitement.

Dottie smiled. "Be right back with the coffees." She took

their menus and went behind the long counter to put in the order.

Finn and Rolf waited for the coffees before starting. Finn looked at the smiling man, picturing him in a berserker rage. He failed to formulate the image. Rolf was too damned smiley. Maybe that was something berserkers did to keep people from knowing the truth. After all, the man smiled constantly.

Dottie put two cups and a beat-up white carafe on the table, along with a sad-looking slice of apple pie. She turned to Rolf. "Food'll be out in a few, hon." She gave him a wink.

Rolf beamed at her. "Thanks, love!"

She chuckled and walked away.

Finn gazed at Rolf. "What just happened?"

Rolf poured a cup of black brew for each of them. "What do you mean?"

"She doesn't like me, but she's sweet on you." Finn lifted the cup and inhaled the rich aroma.

"You try too hard." Rolf took a quick sip and smacked his lips. "You have to know your audience. Dottie works second and third shifts in a twenty-four hour greasy spoon, man. Imagine the shit she has to deal with: drunks, bums, depressed insomniacs, she gets 'em all. She wants to talk as little as possible and get her job done so she can go home and soak her feet. You go and ask her to make a decision for some guy she just met. Just say what you want, man."

Finn glanced at Dottie as she leaned into the kitchen window and spoke to the cook. "You're smarter than you let on, Rolf."

Rolf smiled, his brilliant white teeth contrasting with his dark skin. "People think I'm an old stoner, but they forget there's a whole life behind the smoke. I mean, I am an old stoner, but I'm also a Peabrain, and magic and smoke go together, man."

Finn didn't argue. "So, where the hell did you go? We were talking at the bar and you disappeared."

"Sorry about that, man. I stepped out to have a smoke and sort of forgot to come back, ya'know?"

"Before you wandered off, you said something about using magic while you were in a rage." Finn leaned in. "I need to know how you do that."

"I know you do. But I need to finish my story. To understand the methods, man." He took another gulp of coffee and refilled the cup. As he was about to open his mouth, Dottie set a huge plate of food in front of him.

"Need anything else, sweetie?"

He looked at the plate with wide eyes, then smiled at her. "This is absolutely perfect, thanks."

She smiled and turned to Finn, her frown returning. "You good, big fella?"

Finn gave a tight smile and nodded. "Perfect. Thanks."

She rolled her eyes at his attempt to mirror Rolf and moseyed away.

Rolf chuckled, one of the eggs already in his mouth. "Still trying too hard. Don't sweat it. First impression can be a killer." He stuffed a fork full of hash browns covered in gravy into his mouth, somehow not getting anything on his face. "Mmm."

"You were saying?" Finn prompted when Rolf seemed to be forgetting their conversation.

"Oh, yeah." He swallowed and took another sip of coffee. "So, after I lost my men, I was done, man. I wanted to die, you know? I dropped my gear and wandered into the jungle. I figured if the enemy didn't kill me, the jungle would."

"I understand that. I've been there."

"I bet." He pointed his fork back and forth between them, flinging bits of hash on the table. "Me and you, we're a lot the same, man. Different races, different classes, different planets, but same."

"Because we're both berserkers."

"Naw, man. Lots of fuckers are berserkers, but they ain't got shit on us. We're the same because we're berserkers who want to be good men. That makes us unique. It also fucks us up when things go bad." He took a few more bites.

Contemplative, Finn took a bite of pie, surprised it tasted better than it looked. He had never thought about why he couldn't continue in the army when all the other berserkers had no problems with their killing orders. He never considered he was a good man. He was a machine. A weapon. No one called an axe moral or good, it was an instrument for hacking other beings into tiny bits.

Rolf was right. Finn wanted to be a good person. He just wasn't sure how to go about it.

"Anyway…" Rolf swallowed another bite. "I was out there, like, three days. I had trenchfoot, I'd fallen down a ravine, banged up my arm, other painful shit. I never slept, just walked, lost in despair. Then I took another step and found myself in a manicured yard. It was a temple, one of those old ones that should have fallen down a thousand years ago. I collapsed." He snapped his fingers. "Woke up a day or two later and this little guy in white robes stood over me. Jin. Little fucker saved my life. I was pissed at him." He drained his second cup of coffee. "Jin was a Buddhist monk, all Zen and shit. So, I ended up staying. I helped clean the temple. Wasn't even a Buddhist temple. We just cleaned it up, man. After a few weeks, we set off and found another one in bad shape and cleaned it up too. We did that shit for months. Backbreaking work, but ol' Jin never said a fucking word."

"Not much of a complainer?"

"I mean he didn't say a word. At all. Ever. As in, we didn't talk."

Finn raised an eyebrow. "Vow of silence?"

Rolf laughed. "That's what I thought, man. Turned out Jin just wasn't much of a talker. Sometime around the second month, he asked me to pass the rice. I about fell dead from shock, man. After that, we talked for days. Mostly me. I had shit to get off my chest. Told him about the rage, the magic. Jin didn't bat an eye. Even when I showed him a little of it. He looked at me like I was an asshole for not using magic to make our work go faster." Rolf grinned at the memory. "Nothing fazed this dude, Finn. Nothing, man. Long story short, he started teaching me about Buddhism. And Zen, in particular."

Finn frowned. "I haven't the best luck when it comes to religion." Thoughts came to mind of temples full of insane priestesses trying to kill him as he liberated items from their vaults.

Rolf waved a hand. "Me neither, brother. But from

those conversations, I discovered the key to controlling the rage." He leaned in. "Want to know what they are?"

"That's why I'm here eating this pie."

"Okay, well, three things you need to know to control that demon." He held up a finger. "One. You need to breathe."

Finn set his fork down. He stared at the old man. "I know how to breathe. I'm doing it right now."

Rolf shook his head. "Naw, man. You need to understand. The rage? It's all physical, a reaction your body creates to keep itself alive in bad situations. You can look up the science, but trust me, you can control the physical, no matter how out of control you feel. Breathe slow and deliberate. It slows your heart rate, keeps the blood from rushing around. It gives you an edge. Puts you in control of how much rage to let out."

Finn wasn't convinced, but he wanted to hear more. "And the second thing?"

Rolf folded his hands in front of his half eaten meal. "The second thing is you have to change the story you tell about yourself."

"What?" Finn wasn't aware he was telling a story.

"It's the small stuff." Rolf took a bite of bacon. "Would you say when you go into a rage you lose control to a degree?"

Finn nodded, knowing that all too well.

"That's a lie. You're telling yourself you're not in control. Change the story. The rage works *for* you, not the other way around. Change the story and repeat it to yourself. Over and over. Like a mantra, man. Get all zen with that shit. Changing your story changes the narrative."

"How will that help me use magic when I'm in a rage? The rage blocks it. Hell, it makes you resistant to direct magical effects. That's not in my head."

"Different things, man. Using magic is in the mind. Being affected by magic is physical. The rage changes you *physically*, but mentally you can control the magic." He shoveled the rest of the food into his mouth and guzzled the last of his coffee.

"There you go. That's the secret." Rolf scooted out of the booth. "Give it a shot before writing it off. That shit saved my life. Could save yours. Maybe your friends." He pulled two crumpled twenties out of his pocket and dropped them on the table. "Pie's on me. Catch you later, man."

"Wait!" Finn held out a hand to stop him. "You said three keys. What's the third one?"

"If all else fails..." Rolf smiled and pulled a joint from his pocket. "Does wonders for your mood." He put the joint between his lips and walked to the door, waving to Dottie before leaving.

## CHAPTER FIFTEEN

Danica and Mila surrounded Finn, both with concerned looks.

"Hey, ladies. What can I do for you?" Finn retreated to the kitchen and set the wooden case on the island counter.

"Are you okay?" Mila stepped closer.

Danica pulled his bomber jacket open and began checking him over. "Are you hurt?"

Finn pulled Danica's hands away. "I'm fine. Why wouldn't I be?"

Mila pointed to the couch. Finn followed her finger and saw Remmy bouncing up and down while playing on her smartphone, a bowl of chips and a beer on the coffee table. She looked happier than he'd ever seen her.

"Ah, Remmy. Has she been any trouble?"

Mila and Danica crossed their arms and gave him identical deadpan stares.

"She has, then?"

Mila rolled her eyes. "She's been a little angel, but who the hell is she?" Her whisper had a growl to it. "She told us you got into a fight in an alley, then wandered off with some other white-haired guy with a long scarf who reeked of 'weird smoke.'"

Finn laughed. "That sums it up. Goblins aren't skilled at getting all the minute details across." He laid a large hand on both their shoulders and gave a comforting squeeze. "I'm fine. Penny saw a couple drunks harassing Remmy. I ran them off, then ran into my buddy Rolf, and we grabbed a bite. Nothing dangerous, promise."

Mila and Danica glanced at one another, frowned, then lowered their eyebrows at him. "Who the fuck is Rolf?" Danica asked, slender arms still crossed.

"He's the guy I was talking to at the bar." He locked on Mila. "Remember? I mentioned him, but he took off before you got back."

Mila pursed her pretty lips. "I remember you saying something about some rando, but I never saw the dude."

They followed Finn as he went to the fridge and pulled out a beer. He twisted the top off, not realizing it wasn't a twist-off cap. With his grip strength, it didn't matter. He opened it and took a swig. "He's not some rando, at least I don't think he is. I don't know what that means. He's a berserker, like me. He said he knew how to control the rage, so I thought I should check it out. Turns out he's just spouting some 'change your feelings and you'll feel better' bullshit."

He took another long drink, then looked for Penny. He spied her perched on the back of the couch, watching Remmy play on the phone. "Penny been there the whole time?"

Mila smiled and peered at the little dragon and goblin.

"No, first thing she did was tell us what was up, but we gave up on that and asked the goblin. Penny brought her snacks and a beer, then found a semi-clean towel and one of your t-shirts in the locker room. She's been by her side since, cheering her on while she plays." Mila smiled. "It's actually been really sweet to watch."

"Yeah, Penny's always liked kids." He chugged the rest of his brew and smacked his lips.

At the same time, Mila had paled. "Kid? She's a child? Penny gave her a beer!"

"Remmy! How old are you?" Finn shouted across the room.

Noticing Finn for the first time, she smiled and waved. "Oh, hey boss. I'm, uh, forty-seven, I think. Why?"

"No reason." He turned to Mila and in a quiet voice said, "You're right, she's a little young for beer."

Mila rolled her eyes and slapped his arm. "Now you're just being an ass."

"Actually," Danica intervened, "goblins are pretty long lived. She's still in her late teens, maybe early twenties."

Finn laughed. "Don't worry. Goblins can eat or drink about anything. They're like goats. They have a very interesting digestive system that filters anything and everything, including alcohol. Remmy could eat a brick of arsenic and be fine."

"Okay." Mila nodded, looking less freaked out. "Not that I mind her being here, but *why* is she here?"

"Needed a place to relax. Remmy has it rough as her tribe's main hunter. I figured we could give her a break, let her use the internet for a while."

Mila frowned. "Then what? Just kick her out?"

"Well, she has to go home eventually. Unless she stays the night. I'm sure she would appreciate that, if you two don't mind."

Danica pulled a pair of beers out of the fridge, handing them to Finn to open instead of getting the bottle opener. "I don't mind," she said, "but Hermin will be here in the morning to teleport us to the cabin. She'll have to leave pretty early." She took her opened beer from Finn, and they clinked their bottles. "Unless you want her to watch the house while were gone?" She took an elf-like sip.

Finn took a dwarf-like 'sip.' "Not a terrible idea, but she needs a shower and her clothes washed. She's a little on the sewer-smelling side. Probably why Penny grabbed a towel and tee from the locker room. Always thinking, that dragon." He set off into the living room and leaned on the couch. "Hey, Remmy."

"What's up, boss?" She didn't look up from her game.

"Do you want to stay tonight? You can sleep here on the couch." He patted the back of the gray sectional. "I can attest to its comfort. We're well-acquainted."

She dropped the phone in her lap, peered at him, and clutched her hands together. "Really?"

Finn nodded. "Yup. But…" He held a finger up to forestall her excitement. "First, you have to take a shower and wash your clothes." He gestured at the washer.

She followed his gaze to the machine tucked into an alcove beside the locker room entrance. "That would be amazing!"

"Penny, you put a towel and some clothes in for her?"

"Chi chi." Penny nodded, still lounging on the couch.

Remmy squealed. She jumped up and pulled her hoodie

and grimy white t-shirt off in one go. She kicked her shoes off and dropped her pants before anyone could stop her.

"Alrighty then," Mila said as everyone averted their eyes.

Finn did the same when she squatted, scooped her things up, and sprinted to the washer. She stood tippytoe and dumped the load in the top, then scurried into the locker room. Finn caught a glimpse of her naked backside before it disappeared around the corner. It shocked him to see intricate tattoos all over her back. He'd never seen a goblin so decorated.

"Well, that was...something." Danica laughed. "I think I'll need another one of these to wash my eyeballs with now." She held up the beer and drank the rest, then headed toward the fridge.

"Bring me one?" Mila said. She walked around the couch and flopped down. "Turns out goblin asses are cuter than mine, and I want to forget that fact."

Finn laughed. "You obviously have never had a good look at your butt."

Mila turned and gave him a cheeky smile. "You say the sweetest things, Finn."

He turned red and quickly finished his beer. "Bring me one too, Danica?"

"Need to forget that last line?" she said from the kitchen.

"Yeah. Something like that." He sighed.

Mila laughed.

# CHAPTER SIXTEEN

Mila accepted the beer and patted the seat beside her. "You going to join us?"

Danica eyed her, then Finn, who had taken the seat beside Mila and was still blushing from his comment. "I think I'll head to my room. I have a book I want to finish before we leave. Finn can cuddle you." She made kissy faces at Mila and jabbed her thumb toward Finn.

Mila looked to see if Finn had seen, but he was avoiding eye contact at the moment and oddly rapt with the label on his bottle.

Mila made an angry face at Danica, who giggled and shooed Mila with her hand as if to say 'go on, get him.' Out loud, she said, "Mila, why don't you tell Finn about what you picked up at the store today?"

Mila's cheeks flushed, and she squirmed on the couch, abruptly aware of the new cheeky panties beneath her pants. "Will you shut the fuck up and go to your room already?"

Danica laughed and waved. "Goodnight, you two. See

you in the morning." She used a singsong voice as she walked to her bedroom.

Mila watched her go, her cheeks red and fist balled up.

"You went to the store? That could have been dangerous."

She turned to see Finn with concern on his face and let out a nervous laugh. "It was fine. Hermin teleported us to the mall, so there wasn't any chance of being followed." She took a sip of beer to cover her embarrassment.

"I suppose that's a pretty safe way of getting there. We should have someone teach Danica that spell. She doesn't have a lot of spells that aren't medical related. Anyway, that's a subject for another time. What did you guys get at the mall?"

Mila took another long drink and glanced away, her cheeks renewing their fire.

"Are you okay? You look flush. Is it the headaches?"

"No. They're less frequent, but I still get a pain here and there." She felt bad for misleading him but no way was she about to discuss the bag of new undergarments in her room. She wanted to kill Danica.

He pulled her shoulder toward him. "Here, lay down. I'll rub your head."

She set her beer on the coffee table and rested her head on his lap. Mila closed her eyes as he started rubbing her scalp and temples. She let out a small groan of pleasure, then situated on her back better.

The pressure of tiny feet on her stomach made her look down.

Penny climbed up on her and plopped down on her abs, resting her small dragon head between her breasts. "Chi?"

Mila patted Penny's side. "You're good. Surprised me is all."

Laying her head back down as Finn continued rubbing, they sat in silence for a few minutes, Remmy's faint singing in the shower the only sound. Mila felt herself drifting off.

"She deserves better," Finn said, his tone low and quiet.

"Who?" Mila asked, her eyes still closed.

"Remmy. Her and her people aren't able to assimilate with normal Peabrain society. Even with a concealment spell, they're too different looking. A few hours at a time is fine, people write it off as an oddity, but they can't live aboveground."

Mila gazed up to see him staring toward the locker room with a pensive expression. She felt a spike of emotion that confused her for a second. It took her a few beats to recognize it, and she realized she felt proud of Finn. Why she should feel pride at his words, she couldn't say. He was talking about something horrible, then it hit her. She was proud that not only did he see the problem, he wanted to do something about it. His empathy and natural leadership was coming to the surface.

"So...what do we do about it?" Mila reached up and stroked his shoulder.

Finn's frown deepened. He peered at her. "I don't know. The problem isn't just with goblins. Most races can mix with Peabrains fine. Look at Danica. You lived with her for years and had no clue. Some of them have other traits, though. Makes normal society a challenge."

"What do you mean?"

"The selkies, for example." He took a drink while still rubbing her head with the other hand. "They don't need a concealment spell. They can shift into human form, but they're a species and don't feel comfortable unless they're together. Sure, they're okay for short periods, but long term, selkies need the pack. So, Kevin gathered them into a gang, which has its own set of problems. Same thing with the orcs and goblins and any other tribal race. For a lot of species, tribal life is a physical need as much as a social one."

Mila observed the pain in Finn's eyes, and she wished she knew how to relieve it. She knew how he felt about the disenfranchised, Finn being an exile himself. He knew what it meant to be unwelcome and unwanted, and he didn't like thinking about others dealing with that same pain.

"How do we help them?"

He stared into her eyes. "You really are something special, you know that?"

Mila blushed.

"That's the problem," he continued. "I don't see how we can help them. There are millions of people across the globe facing these same issues. That's why the Dark Star's message is gaining steam. The problem is too big for one dwarf to fix."

They were homing in on something familiar. Mila had volunteered for plenty of causes over the years, giving her a frame of reference for this kind of problem. "That's just it," she said. "It *is* too big to fix. If you look at it on a global scale. Like you said, you're one dwarf. You need to think smaller at first." She pointed to the locker room where Remmy's warbling voice accompanied the running water. "In there right now is a goblin girl taking her first shower in a long time, and from the sound of it, loving every second. You changed something today for *her*."

Finn nodded, staring off, deep in thought. "Yeah, but it's only temporary."

"Shir shi, chi?" Penny lifted her head and cocked it.

"That's a good idea," Mila said, her eyes going wide. "We could start buying properties. That way we can help the ones that can't work regular jobs. It's a start, right?" Mila smiled at Penny.

Finn gave them both an odd look.

"What?" she said. "Is that a dumb idea?"

He glanced back and forth between them, then shook his head. "No, it's a great idea. Penny's pretty smart."

He was hinting at something, but Mila didn't follow. Finn sighed when he saw she wasn't getting it. "Good thing Penny *said* something. Right?"

Mila lifted her head to stare at Penny, who returned the stare. "I understood you! Not like the little bits from context, but actually understood you! Say something else."

"Shir chi shee?" Penny gazed at her, a smile on her face.

Mila frowned. "Say it again."

"Shir. Chi. Shee." The tiny dragon enunciated each word.

Mila shook her head and let it drop into Finn's lap. "What the fuck? How can I understand her one second then nothing the next?"

Finn stroked her hair. "Don't worry too much about it. Her language is beyond difficult and uses a lot of magic to get the meaning across. This is a good thing. It means you have access to at least a small bit of your peabrain."

"I suppose that is good news." She tilted her head and

smiled at him. "You do know how to make me feel better. Don't you, you big charmer?"

He laughed. "Well, I might be a charmer, but I just had a thought. We will need to ward any place we buy to keep the occupants safe and unnoticed, which can take a lot of time, since right now, Penny is our only warder."

"Chi chi!" Penny nodded wearily.

"I know, it takes a lot out of you, and we appreciate all the work," Finn said, before turning his gaze to Mila. "So, what if we start with this building? We could buy the whole thing and start renovating the condos for group living. The occupants would be safe, and we would have people to watch our backs. Maybe even set up some work-shops so the tenants could make some extra money selling stuff. I know the selkies have a couple of good businesses. They could teach others."

Mila thought it might be odd to have a bunch of magi-cals as neighbors, but she saw the advantages. People watching their backs sounded great, what with all the assassins and mercs coming after them.

"I love it." Mila lifted a hand and stroked his cheek. "Let's do it."

Finn smiled and vibrated with renewed energy. Mila marveled at the change in him from a minute ago. He might not realize it, but she could see plain as day, he needed to help those in need. It was how he dealt with injustice in the world. He was a true prince.

He was *her* prince.

The words came out before she could stop them. "Do you want to go out?"

He furrowed his brow at her. "What?"

She felt her face redden. What was it she had told him when they first met? In for a penny, in for a pound. "On a date. You want to go on a real date with me?"

His face sobered, and a smile appeared. "You want to go on a date with me?"

"Why wouldn't I?"

He gazed across the room at nothing. "I'm not a good person, Mila."

She laughed. "Are you kidding me? You just decided to buy a whole building to provide for those less fortunate to give them a home. If that's not good, I don't know what is."

He brushed a stray lock of hair from her face. "I've done terrible things. Things that would change your opinion of me."

She gave him a stern look and laid a hand on his cheek. "We all have a past, Finn. Things we don't want others to know about, things we think would ruin us if they ever got out. That doesn't change who we are. Everyone's fucked up. Everyone has shame and doubt and fear. That doesn't make us less. It makes us more."

"You don't understand…"

She sat up, placing Penny on her lap and sitting cross-legged facing Finn. She put a hand on both his cheeks, making him look at her. "You were used by your father as a weapon. You're right, I don't know the details, but I don't have to. I know you're a good man because you walked away from that life knowing you would lose everything, and you did it anyway."

He gazed at her with eyes deeper than the ocean and full of a dark past.

Mila's heart broke for him, but he needed to see he

wasn't that person anymore. "Since the day I met you, you've been nothing but kind and respectful to me and everyone around you. You *are* good. The only one who doesn't believe it is you. We love you. Me, Penny, Danica, hell, I'm willing to bet money Remmy loves you too. It's time you loved yourself."

She gazed at him and, as the time drew out, his eyes softened. A slight smile touched his face, and he put his hands on hers, guiding them from his face to his lap. "You're right. The past is the past. Not much I can do about it now. I need to move forward from who I was and become someone new."

"Not *become* someone new, Finn. You already are. Now you need to forgive yourself so you can heal. Carrying your past is like trying to run a marathon with a big bleeding gash in your thigh. You're not going to get far. It has to heal first."

"You're pretty smart, Dr. Winters."

She gave him a huge smile.

"Okay, so how do I do that?"

"By taking me out on a date, you big idiot."

He laughed, and she leaned in and wrapped her arms around his neck. They smiled at one another for a few seconds. "Now would be an excellent time to kiss me, in case you were wondering," she whispered.

And, for the first time, they truly kissed. Not a good luck kiss or a pre-battle jitters peck or because they thought they might die. It was a kiss meant to be a kiss, purely and deeply, and Mila lost herself in it.

"Hey, boss, I can come back after the hanky panky, if you want," Remmy said.

Mila and Finn's eyes opened at the same time. Mila backed away, putting some distance between them to look at Remmy, her white hair still wet. She wore one of Finn's black t-shirts big as a dress or a nightgown, and she shifted on her feet beside the couch, unsure what she should do.

Finn and Mila regarded one another then burst out laughing.

"Have a seat, Remmy," Mila said.

"Yeah. No hanky panky going on, whatever that is," Finn added.

Mila gave him a sly look. "Not tonight, anyway."

The room filled with Penny's and Mila's laughter at Finn's sudden deer-in-headlights expression.

## CHAPTER SEVENTEEN

Settled onto the couch, Remmy began playing her game again, unaware of the significance of what she had interrupted. Finn's shirt looked like an oversized dress on her tiny frame, even the short sleeves were down around her wrists.

Finn half-wanted to strangle the little goblin and half-wanted to thank her. He glanced at Mila's flush face. She was draining the last of her beer, although her eyes gazed sidelong at him. After the bottle came away from her lips, she smiled.

No one had ever seen his fears like she had, and she still wanted more of him. Maybe he *had* been selling himself short. He would work hard to be the man she believed him to be. On that note, he decided they should get back to the matter they had been discussing earlier.

"How would we go about buying the building?" he asked and sipped from his bottle.

"I have no idea," Mila said, more comfortable now that he was moving the conversation along. "I winged it with the condo. We need someone who knows how to even begin."

"Squee chir chi," Penny said from her lap, glancing between Mila and Finn.

Finn raised an eyebrow. "You have a personal assistant?"

"Personal assistant?" Mila mimicked, looking at Penny. "You have a personal assistant?"

"Shir shee shee. Chi chi."

Finn laughed, and Mila waited for a translation. "She hired an assistant for us. Technically, they work for the goldmine we set up. Her name is Grace, and she's been helping Penny acquire some hard-to-find gear." He pulled out his phone and handed it to Penny, who navigated the menus and pulled up the contact, which was already entered in his phone. He took it and raised an eyebrow. "She knows who I am?"

Penny nodded and pointed to Mila. "Shee shir."

"She said you have this Grace's contact info on your phone as well."

Mila pulled her phone from her pocket and scrolled it as Finn composed a text. He appreciated being able to communicate without having to talk in person. He mouthed words as he thumbed the screen, so they would know what he was typing. "Hello, Grace. This is Finn. Penny said she hired you to be our assistant. I need to find out how to buy our condo building and all the condos in it right away." He hit send, put the phone down, and grinned. "Probably won't hear back for a whi—"

The phone chimed. He glanced at a reply. "Hello, Finn. Good to meet you! Penny has said great things. I can start the paperwork to buy the building and set up a negotiation for the price with the owners. What is the max you want to spend?"

He stared at the screen. "Well, shit. That was fast." He replied he would leave the amount up to her, but he would like to get the building quick as possible.

Penny gave him a smug look. "Squee chi, shir?"

"You're right. She's good. We should have hired her a long time ago." He gave her a fist bump.

"I still can't believe you hired an assistant." Mila reeled from the revelation, even if Finn was used to Penny doing things like this without him. "How do you communicate? I assume she doesn't speak dragon."

"Chi shir." Penny mimicked typing.

"Wait…you type in English?" Mila shook her head to clear it. "Of course you do. Why didn't I think of that? You're on the internet constantly. You would have to know how to write English. Why didn't we think of this? We can really speed up the process of me learning your language."

Penny waggled a hand in a 'kind of' motion.

"Penny's language is magical," Finn explained. "A typed translation won't really help because there's not much meaning to the sounds she makes without the magic. Thats why our ears only hear a handful of sounds when she speaks." Finn didn't like seeing Mila's defeated expression. "But hey, still a great way to communicate in a pinch."

"I suppose so." Mila leaned back on the couch, then her eyes widened at Remmy.

Finn glanced over. The goblin was rolling up the sleeves on the t-shirt, which exposed the tattoos on her upper arms and shoulders.

"Holy shit, Remmy," Mila exclaimed. "Those are some amazing tattoos."

Remmy dropped the phone in her hands and pulled her sleeve up over her shoulder. "You like? I earned them all! Only our leader has more, and he is old and stuff."

"I've never seen tattoos on a goblin before," Finn remarked. On his homeworld, goblins were fanatics about remaining pure to serve their lord better or something like that. Goblins tattooing themselves fascinated him. "Why do you do it?"

Remmy jumped off the couch and, in one quick motion, her shirt was on the floor. She turned her backside to them with a comical disregard for her nudity. She twisted her arm around and pointed to where a large tribal symbol dominated her spine above the small of her back to below her shoulder blades. The intricate art spiraled to form a larger design that swept across her back and over her shoulders and thighs and ended as it wrapped around her arms and legs.

"This is our emblem." Her finger jabbed at the center of her back. "Everyone has one." She ran her finger along one of the swirls away from the central design. "Each of these is for a big time deed. I killed six dire rats and saved a child for this. And this one is for when I traded pelts with a mage at the Market and brought extra food."

"That's amazing." Finn smiled. Remmy was proud of her ink—as she should be—but it still confused him why they did it. "Why do you document your deeds like this?"

She turned and looked questioning. Her nudity made him a tad edgy, but he kept his gaze on her out of respect.

"We don't have a master to keep track of them, so is the best thing we could think of when the last dwarf lord died."

"You serve dwarves?" Mila asked. Her face was still red, whether from the kissing or Remmy's display, Finn had no clue. "I don't understand. Why would you serve them if you don't have to?"

Finn knew Remmy's reply wouldn't make sense to Mila. "Where we're from, goblins and dwarves live together," he told her. "Their species is subservient...part of the problem we were talking about. A tribe attaches to a family line of dwarves and serves them. They rank themselves amongst the other tribes by how powerful their patron is. It's an odd social structure, but without dwarves here on Earth, they have to find another way to establish the ranking system. It looks like Remmy's tattoos are their solution."

"Yup, the boss understands." Remmy remained on full display, glancing back and forth between them, not giving a flying fuck they could see all her bits.

Mila cleared her throat. "So, um, whats your favorite tattoo?"

Remmy's eyes brightened. She lifted her leg, planting a foot on the couch right in front of Mila, and pointed to one that went from her knee to the bottom of her torso. It appeared newer, looking darker and more defined than the others. "This one I got when I found the boss, and he introduced us to the Naga. A big day for our tribe." She beamed at Finn, her sharp white teeth in a grin that nearly split her face.

"The Naga?" Mila raised an eyebrow.

He waved her off. "It's no big deal. I'll tell you later."

Mila nodded and turned to Remmy. She shook her

head. "Fuck me, Remmy. You look like one of those crossfit badasses. Do you even have an ounce of fat on you?"

Remmy stepped back and struck a bodybuilder pose to put on a gun show. "Gotta stay fit to protect the tribe. I'm the best warrior we have."

Finn glanced at the goblin, not knowing what crossfit was. Every muscle in Remmy's compact form had definition. She was cut like few people can achieve without dehydration, with a well-defined eight pack of abs under her taut green skin. The sight, while impressive, saddened Finn. Most goblins he had come across were in fine shape, but nothing to this extreme. Another sign of how hard she must work to protect her people in a hostile environment. No wonder she was over the moon to have a night where she could relax.

Finn snatched the t-shirt from the floor and held it toward Remmy. "Arms up," he commanded, and she jabbed her arms straight up. He put the shirt over her head, making sure to roll the sleeves so her hands and arms were free. "Your tattoos are impressive. Thanks for showing us."

"No problem, boss." Remmy smiled, playing with the front of the shirt between her fingers.

"We have a long day tomorrow," Mila said after finishing her beer. "We should get to bed. The couch is yours, Remmy. Grab some pillows and blankets on the shelf over there. Do you need anything before we go?"

Remmy leapt forward and wrapped her arms around Mila's neck in a tight hug. "No. I'm great. Thanks for letting me stay the night."

Mila hugged back, patting her a few times. "It's our pleasure, sweetheart."

The goblin faced Finn and bowed. "Thanks, boss."

Finn scooped her up in a hug as well, lifting her off her feet from his seated position. "Anytime, Remmy. You can feel at ease here. If you need anything, just knock on my door."

# CHAPTER EIGHTEEN

Finn snorted awake. He scanned the dark room, finding the clock Mila had put beside his bed. 6:02 am. "Ugh." With a groan, he went to stuff his head under his pillow then realized a ringing phone was what woke him. He felt the soft nothingness of sleep and relaxed his grip on the pillow. Another ring jarred him to wakefulness.

"Alright, already," he roared into the pillow before throwing it across the room. He snatched his phone up and stabbed the green answer button with a finger. "What?"

"Finn." Preston Meriwether's smooth baritone came over the line. "Did I catch you at a bad time?"

"It's six in the morning, Preston." Finn felt his throat crunching out the words as he worked his vocal chords for the first time that day.

"Yes, it is. I figured you would have been up for at least an hour already. Aren't you heading to the lake this morning?"

Finn swung his feet out of bed and flexed his toes on the hardwood floor. "Yeah. We're leaving in an hour.

What can I do for you?" Finn felt his irritation rising, even if it was only twenty minutes before he intended to awaken.

"I wanted to let you know what's been happening around the world, and how it might impact your operation."

Preston paused, which irritated Finn further, since there wasn't much to say to that yet. Preston got the idea when Finn softly growled.

"Most major cities are seeing an uptick in violence against magicals. The source is unknown, but we both know the Dark Star is to blame. The magical communities don't understand her tactics and so far their outcry for support is not being met. Rather, they are turning to the Dark Star for a solution, seeing as she is promising a magical nation out in the open for all to see."

"I figured that would happen." Finn's rage was beginning to awaken too. "Is it out of control?"

"No, not yet." It sounded like Preston took a sip of tea. "Graffiti of the Dark Star's symbol has been spotted in many of the affected cities. Support for her is on the rise. I'm deploying all G.A.E.L. forces at my disposal to lend aid where possible."

"All right. That's good." Finn paused, then said, "Why are you telling me this?"

"I need you to understand, Finn, I can't offer support from my end for your excursion." At least some earnest frustration came through in his voice.

"So, you called to tell me you're not helping. Like the last time with the hounds?" His rage had its coffee and surged through him now. He opened his mouth to yell at

Preston for wasting his time when an image of Rolf's smiling face flashed in his mind.

Finn decided the old stoner's method was worth a try. He sucked a deep breath and let it out, waited a second, then did it again. Finn closed his eyes, feeling for the rage and its intense heat. He latched onto it, breathed again and forced calm to take hold. After a dozen breaths, Finn opened his eyes. He was shocked. The rage was cooling.

Preston had been talking, but Finn was so thrilled by how he just kept the rage in check he hadn't heard a word. "Sorry, Preston. I appreciate the update. I'll do my best to resolve the issue with the *Anthem* on our own. I hope G.A.E.L. can do some good out there. Bye."

He ended the call before Preston responded. Rolf's simple technique worked. Finn smiled and dropped his phone on the bed. If the breathing thing worked, maybe the whole "changing the story" thing would too.

Rolf had been right. Finn spoke about himself in a defeatist language, saying things like the rage *took* him, instead of the rage *happening* inside him. He was focusing on the negatives instead of the positives. It was such a foreign concept, he didn't know where to go with it.

His phone rang again. He'd been abrupt with Preston, so maybe he was calling back. He answered without looking. "Hey Preston, I'm sor—"

A sultry female voice cut him off. "Having troubles with the cow, are we, Finnegan?"

Finn narrowed his eyes and checked the caller ID. An unavailable number. He put the phone back to his ear. "Who is this?"

The voice chuckled. "Oh, come now. I'm insulted you'd

even ask. I must say you really threw a wrench in my works when you captured Jeffery. He was such a useful tool with his knowledge of dwarven artifacts."

"You got the tool part right." Finn frowned. "What do you want... I'm not calling you 'Dark Star,' that's idiotic. What's your name?"

She chuckled without humor. "Dark Star is my title. You may call me Hellena."

"Hellena?" Such a normal name. Then again, should it not have been? "What is it you want from me? Besides being dead. I appreciate the high bounty, by the way. Really shows my worth."

"Oh, my dear prince," she cooed. "The bounty is for your capture, not your death. I wouldn't kill the last dwarf on Earth. You are far too valuable."

"But you're willing to kill my friends?"

"They are holding you back. You could be so much more by my side. I'm sure you have seen the squalor so many of our people need to suffer to exist in this world the Peabrains have corrupted. We could save them, our kind. Give them a place to belong. That is more than that cow Meriwether can do."

"And you think killing my friends is the way to win me over?"

"I think you are a man who sees the big picture. Surely your family uses such tactics on those they wish to influence. It is all part of the game, Finnegan." Her capricious manner irked him, as if talking about killing people to make him notice her was merely a warm up.

"Your dark magic must have addled your brain if you think I would ever help you."

"And why is that? There are many who will perish if the world is to know what is under their noses. Finnegan, I don't want to hurt your friends, but you're leaving me with little choice. You keep interfering with my plans, and someone needs to pay for these drawbacks."

"You're mad. Coming out in the open and taking land to start your own country will lead to nothing but war. The Peabrains won't stop until you or they are dead. You hear me? You can't win this way."

She laughed, high and staccato. "Oh, Finnegan. We have nothing to fear from them. They have forgotten their power. Like children sent to battle with only their hands, they stand no chance against a united magical nation. If you come to my side, we could spare them. I have a weapon that will cull even the most determined human. Their governments will tremble at its use. A weapon—"

"The Gjallarhorn. Yeah, I heard. Let me guess, you want me to use it to scare them into line?"

For a few beats, he heard nothing but silence, then the sultry voice returned. "You are better informed than I gave you credit for."

Finn felt some pride for having surprised her. "I also know you can't use it without me. You may as well throw that thing into a volcano for all the good it will do. I'll never blow that horn for you."

"Don't be so sure of your ancestors' cleverness," she chided in a singsong voice. "Many follow me who are clever in their own rights. Very soon, we will break the locks that hold the Gjallarhorn at bay."

"Then why do you want me by your side? You have it all figured out."

"I am not so foolish to think I am infallible. I am a pragmatist and having the last living dwarf by my side, a royal one at that, goes far in convincing our community to follow us to a new world. Think of the humans, Finnegan. Don't you want to save those who cannot save themselves? You seem to have such a compassionate streak." She purred the last sentence.

"I'll tell you what, Hellena. Take the bounties down, and I'll consider helping you out."

She laughed. "Why would I do that? Then you have no motivation to come to me. A little pressure buoys the soul. Really brings things to the surface, don't you think? Gets things done."

It was a longshot, but he felt he had to try. She was right. He was looking to take some pressure off. "Sorry, Hellena. I don't side with crazy."

She gave a theatrical sigh. "Very well. I'll give you another couple weeks of dodging assassins to reconsider. In the end, I always get what I want. It's a shame your friends will have to teach you that lesson with their lives."

The call ended. He tossed the phone onto his bed and got dressed with a scowl. One good thing had come from the conversation, though. She didn't know they knew where the *Anthem* was, or that they were on their way to it.

# CHAPTER NINETEEN

F inn strode into the dojo. To his surprise, everyone was already waiting.

Danica held a duffel bag in one hand, with her bow and quiver over her shoulder, and a backpack that bulged in odd ways. She wore thick, black winter leggings and knee-high black snow boots with black fur around the top. On top, she wore a puffy white coat with the hood up, framing her face with a rim of white fur.

Mila was in her usual tights, a maroon sweater with her belt over top, and a pair of chunky boots that looked like they could kick a door in with no trouble. He could see she had a matching white puffy coat to Danica's, but hers was on the table beside her duffel. He smiled when he saw Penny perched on Mila's shoulder, happy the dragon had taken to her.

Along with the girls, the selkie twins stood with their backs to Finn, dressed for the cold in matching brown Carhartt overalls and thick leather boots. They chattered with Hermin, who, as always, wore grease-stained cover-alls. They had their heads close, and the Huldu used animated gestures as he spoke.

"Good morning, everyone," Finn said, raising an eyebrow. "Did I miss something?"

They all turned at once, then rushed over. Hermin said, "The trees are in an uproar," as if that meant something to Finn.

"Okay. Is it another group of elves growing more super-trees again?"

Hermin paused a sec with a puzzled look. "Eh? Oh. No, not that. The trees up at Grand Lake are worrying. They called one of the elementals to their aid, but it'll be a while before he gets there. You need to stop the leaks from the *Anthem*. That piece of junk is spewing raw magic into the water. It's causing all sorts of chaos, corrupting the land and whatnot. Soon it will affect the wildlife." He frowned. "We should have blown that damn ship up when we had the chance."

"You did," Finn reminded him. "It just wasn't soon enough. But the *Anthem* shouldn't be corrupting anything. It uses pure magic to power it. Letting it vent should only increase the area's magical potential, not contaminate it."

"Well, something is buggering up the works. We can't do much about getting rid of the ship since it's right beside a town." He rubbed a hand down his face. "If we try to blow it up again, it would take the town with it, and something that big is too hard to move, especially since it's at the bottom of a lake. I don't know how the Dark Star managed it in the first place, to be honest."

"I know it sounds impossible, but I think we can disable the ship and keep it from leaking or venting or whatever the hell those idiots are doing to it." Finn put a reassuring hand on Hermin's shoulder.

"Are you all ready?" he asked the selkies and Danica.

All three nodded.

"Good, so we need you to lay low. Get the cabin situated, see if you can see where the Dark Star's people are. Under no circumstances should you leave the protective spells of the cabin. And be sure to have the key on you or the house will reject you, whatever that means. Preston was unclear on that, and we don't want anyone finding out the hard way."

The three stepped close to Hermin, bags in their hands.

"Hermin, thanks for this. We owe you," Finn said with a wave.

"I don't know. By my calculations, I'd say we're about even," the Huldu said with a grin. "Take care of this, and me and Garret will owe *you* one."

Hermin held out his hand and golden light trickled from it like falling glitter. The rich smell of earth filled the condo, and a huge bubble appeared around all four of them. In the blink of an eye, it popped, and they vanished.

The earthy smell dissipated as Finn glanced at Mila watching the empty space.

"That will never get old," she said, crossing over to the table and looking over her and Finn's bags. "You ready? It's a long drive up the mountain. I hope they've cleared the roads. The Hellcat isn't exactly winter-friendly."

A snore cut the air like a buzzsaw through wood. Finn

looked over the back of the couch at Remmy sprawled out, deep asleep. She had removed the t-shirt during the night and was butt-ass naked. He chuckled and pulled the blanket from the back of the couch to cover her up.

"I'm ready, but I want to give you something first." He strode to the kitchen and retrieved the wooden case he'd left on the counter last night. He returned and set it on the table in front of her. "Something you said yesterday got me thinking."

"Open it?"

He gestured at it, and she opened the case and gasped. "Finn. A gun?"

"You said we may as well get you one. It wasn't a bad idea."

"I was joking. I was frustrated about my training, that's all. I...I don't have a permit to carry this."

"It's not a regular gun." He reached into the case and pulled the pistol out of the black leather holster and showed her the various details. "See? Doesn't have a hammer or a magazine. In the hands of a Peabrain, this is, like, a replica."

Penny leaned over from Mila's shoulder. "Chi, chi."

"Yeah, Penny. A magic pistol. It's called an Ivar. Look, it doesn't even need ammo."

"Then what good will it do me?" Mila raised her eyebrow. "I'm just a Peabrain, unless you forgot that little fact."

He lowered a tight stare on her. "This gun is a great way to test your abilities. It uses raw potential magic. Unlike the circlet, it won't pull for magic that's not there. Plus, it uses a fraction of the amount the circlet tried to take. It will either work or not, but it shouldn't damage you. We can try it when we get to the lake. I thought it might be a nice addition to your arsenal."

She accepted the pistol from him with a look of doubt on her face. "None of you have felt any kind of magic from me. What makes you think I'll suddenly get some from somewhere?"

"That's just it. We don't detect any magic from you, *but* you keep doing things that are clearly magical in nature." He pointed to Penny. "Like randomly understanding Penny. That isn't possible without magic. You can talk to bugs. Also not natural. You sometimes see through illusions, like at the house with the hounds or my tattoos." He pointed to the side of his head. "All of those things require magic, Mila. And you do them, even if it's only some of the time. There is magic in you. For whatever reason, we can't detect it, but it's there."

Mila smiled. She tested the gun's weight, then peered at Finn. "How is it possible?"

"Maybe a different kind of magic?"

Penny gasped, and Mila glanced at her. "What?"

"Squee, shir shi chi?"

Finn shrugged. "I don't know what kind of magic. Hell, could be something new, from the Earth, who knows. All I know is where there's smoke, there's fire. And you put off a buttload of smoke for someone not on fire...well, you know what I mean."

"You two think I'm, what, something new?"

"Maybe. You could be. No point stressing over it

though." He put a reassuring hand on her shoulder. "We'll face it together. Who knows, you might like the ride."

She gave him an uneasy smile. "Yeah, maybe."

She didn't sound all that sure, but Finn trusted fate would work it out.

# CHAPTER TWENTY

Finn helped Mila attach the Ivar pistol to the back of her weapon belt. He made sure it was in a proper place for her to reach it or Gram without either getting in the way of her fetching the one she wanted. When the harness and holster were situated, Finn helped her into her puffy coat.

Another snore tore through the condo.

Finn grinned at Mila and walked to the couch. Remmy looked more peaceful than he had ever seen her. He hated to wake her.

"You know, it might be good to have her stay and look after the condo while we're gone."

Mila shrugged, looking at Remmy as she stepped next to Finn.

"Shir shee," Penny said from her shoulder, before jumping up to Finn's for a better view.

"Penny's right. Remmy won't want to stay away from her tribe."

Mila bit her lip. "If they all came here, could we trust

them not to steal everything, or destroy the place? I don't know anything about goblins. Is that a bad idea?"

Finn chuckled. "Not *per se*, but they can get rambunctious. I think Remmy could keep them in line, though, *if* she wasn't pranking us about her tattoos. Sounds like she's respected by her tribe."

Mila smiled at the sleeping goblin. "They all deserve a good shower and a meal. We built a locker room for this kind of thing." She peered at Finn. "May as well get a bunch of goblins to test it out for us."

"Okay, but if we come back and the place looks like they had a party for a few days, it's because they did." Finn reached down, grabbed Remmy's big toe, and gave it a shake. "Time to get up, Remmy."

The blanket flew into the air, and the goblin went from sleeping to standing on the couch in a fighting stance in less than a second. "I'll fuckin' cut you!" The sweet innocent face had turned feral. Then she realized it was them and dropped into a crosslegged position, yawned, and rubbed her eyes. Her white hair stood up in all directions. "Morning already…" She yawned again.

Finn blinked, recovering from Remmy's lightning reflexes. He barked a laugh. "We were hoping you and your tribe might stay here and keep an eye on the condo for us while we're gone."

Remmy stopped rubbing her face and stared at him. "You serious, boss? Not pullin' my leg? Or my toe?"

Mila piped up. "Rules. First, everyone needs to shower right away *and* clean their clothes. I don't want to need a new couch because this one's covered in grime. And, second, keep everyone in line. You can use the TV and the kitchen and what not, but stay out of our rooms and, for the love of god, don't even think about going into Danica's room. She will eat you alive if you mess with her stuff."

Remmy nodded along as if all Mila's rules were a given. "So we can stay?"

"Can you keep the place clean? And your people in line?" Mila asked.

Remmy popped up and gave them both a salute. "You know I can, boss and boss. If anyone gets out of line, I'll beat their asses good. Pow!"

Finn nodded at Mila.

"Okay, then," she said. "Your tribe can stay here."

Remmy clapped her hands and grinned. "Thank you so much, boss! I'll keep em in line. Promise."

Remmy solemnly took Finn's hand. They shook. Then she reached out and shook Mila's hand too. "It's a promise!"

"Now," Mila said, "you should put some clothes on. I think we've seen about as much of your naked ass as we can take."

"You got it, boss!"

---

Finn stood in the alley as Mila pulled the Charger out of the garage and into a fresh three inches of snow that had coated everything overnight. Even in that short distance, the tires spun twice.

Finn opened the trunk and dropped their bags in, making sure the duffel Penny made them bring was secure since the dragon told him it was full of delicate equipment.

He had no clue how a tiny dragon could need so much stuff, but she was rarely wrong, so he did as asked.

Mila rolled the driver's window down and stuck her head out. "This drive is going to be hell. I had snow tires put on, but this fucking car is too charged up for snow. We should take Danica's Forester."

Finn held up a finger and dug into his bomber jacket. "I have an idea." He procured a box of Charleston Chews and popped the top, dumping a few into his hand. Penny tapped him on the head from her spot on his shoulder, and he handed the box to her.

"That's your idea? Have a Chew? Brilliant."

He chuckled. "No, the Chews are a happy accident." He pulled a piece of purple chalk from his pocket. "I was going after this."

"How will that help?"

He smiled, still chewing, and bent to the closest tire. Finn made an intricate rune set, then closed his eyes and funneled power into it. Satisfied, he moved to the next. After a few minutes, he had rune-marked all four tires. He took the half-empty box of Charleston Chews from Penny and made a face at her. She stuck out a chocolate-covered tongue at him as he climbed into the car.

"Okay, give that a try." He reached over his shoulder and fastened his safety belt.

She hit the accelerator. Rather than spin out like before, it rocketed forward. When she stomped on the brake, the car stopped immediately instead of sliding.

"What did you do? Oh, shit! Fuck me, that's insane!" Mila stared out the windshield and grinned. "We stuck to the road like glue."

"I bound the metal in the tires to the stone of the Earth. It has limits, and will only last a few days, but until it wears off, we won't be slipping or sliding anywhere. Congratulations, you now have a snow-worthy muscle car."

She bounced in her seat like a kid in a candy shop. "Holy shit, Finn. This will take some getting used to but it's awesome!" She pulled onto the snowy street and gunned it. The Charger surged forward like they were on a summer highway. "When we stop to gas up, you're getting whatever snacks you want."

"I like snacks."

"Chi chi!"

# CHAPTER TWENTY-ONE

When they stopped for gas and snacks on the edge of town, Finn caught sight of a white panel van pull in after them. He figured more bounty hunters, but kept his trap shut. He didn't want to scare Mila, and once they hit the open road, they'd leave the morons in the dirt. Or the snow, in this case.

As suspected, the bounty hunters lurked and watched, either gathering their courage or waiting for a less populated area to make a move. No one accosted them while they filled up on gas and processed foods. As soon as they were past city limits, Mila stepped on it. Finn had a grand time watching the van try to keep up, lose control, and spin off the road a half-mile behind them.

The Hellcat roared along Route 40. Mila kept the car around seventy and grinned the whole way. Finn couldn't help but smile at her exuberance and spent most of the trip watching her. They had been tail-free ever since the gas station, and he relaxed once they got halfway to Grand Lake. After a series of switchbacks, they broke through the low cloud cover and were nearly blinded by the sun. Mila put on a pair of aviator shades.

The roads were still covered in snow, but from its slushy composition, it had fallen hours ago before the thick clouds had poured into the valley and onto the plains beyond.

Mila pointed to a pulloff overlooking the valley they'd been climbing out of for the last twenty miles. "I need to stretch my legs, and the view from here has to be spectacular."

They pulled into a snow-covered parking area at the side of the road. A big brown sign read BertHound Pass Trailhead. A small outhouse-style toilet and a standing board with information and trail maps were beyond the sign.

Mila shut the car off, stretching her arms across her chest a couple times. "Ready?" she asked, pulling the door handle and climbing out. She shivered and reached into the backseat for her puffy coat. "Got cold quick up here."

Finn climbed out and stretched his back, feeling it pop in a few places. "Man, that feels good." He groaned and noticed Penny doing the same thing while standing on the passenger seat.

"Chi. Chi." She whipped her long neck, and it cracked all the way up.

The move always made Finn queasy, hearing so many vertebrae pop like popcorn. So, of course, Penny did it when he was watching. "You're such an asshole," he said, and she snickered, then hopped into the air and onto his shoulder.

Mila did some standing stretches, reaching down and

pulling her nose to her knees, giving Finn an unintentional show...though the smile on her face told him it might not be unintentional.

He gazed around. They had risen above the heavy snow clouds in the city and enjoyed a clear view over the cloud tops. Finn sucked in a chill breath and reveled at the stinging cold in his lungs. A forest pine scent filled the air, reminding him of his magic.

The wet slushy noise of the occasional car crawling by on their way up the mountain was the only sound except for the far away *whump-whump* of a helicopter somewhere in the valley below.

Finn walked over next to Mila, who had her hands in her pockets, her hood down as she gazed with wonder over the majestic snow-draped mountain forests and billowing sea of clouds.

"Have you ever seen anything so beautiful?" she asked, a smile on her face.

He was about to say 'yes, you,' but felt it was far too cheesy and stopped himself. He peered over the vista, trying to recall a sight so amazing from his travels, yet nothing came to mind. "This is truly a magnificent ship. The entire thing is built to show off the wonders of the universe all in one place." He sucked in another breath and closed his eyes, soaking in the sun.

The *whumping* of the helicopter grew louder, though still distant. Finn scanned the sky, but either it was obscured by the sun or the mountains were bouncing the copter's noise. Something about it was odd, as if it were coming from below them. Finn strode to the edge of the pulloff parking area and searched over the side of the mountain. Thick white clouds clung to the rock a few dozen feet below, limiting what he could see, yet the sound of the rotors kept increasing.

"Must be someone who didn't want to drive through the snow." Mila stepped next to him to peep over the edge. "Probably heading up to Grand Lake, too. Lots of well-off people have second homes there."

"People like Preston Meriwether?"

She smiled, the aviators giving her an official look that fit her well. "I'm pretty sure there aren't any other people like Preston."

"You might be surprised. I bet a lot of wealthy people are magica—"

The muffled sound became a sudden roar as a Black Hawk helicopter shot up out of the clouds, hugging the mountain not twenty feet in front of them. Finn and Mila stumbled back, putting their hands up to block the snow and pebbles whizzing their way.

The matte black chopper had no markings whatsoever on it. It leveled even with them and presented its broad side. Four men in black tactical gear pointed rifles their way from the open side hatch.

"Hands up or we open fire!" a voice said from a loudspeaker. "Back away from the edge. Don't even think about running. Nobody can outrun a bullet. Understand?"

Finn raised his hands and felt Penny slide out of sight down his back. He watched Mila start to reach into her coat, presumably for the gun, and he shook his head. She reluctantly raised her hands, and they both stepped back.

The Black Hawk swooped to the side and set down. The four shooters piled out followed by three more. They all kept their rifles trained on them as they spread out in a semicircle. When they were covered, an eighth man stepped out, also wearing tactical gear and an air of being in charge. He kept his rifle at his side on its strap as he marched toward them.

"You've got a lead foot, missy. When you lost us in the city, we had to scramble quick." He had a southern drawl and had to shout over the whine of the turbines. "Lucky for us, by then we knew you were on 40 with very few turnoffs. Imagine my surprise when you stopped here to enjoy the view, giving us the perfect opportunity."

"Who the fuck are you?" Finn shouted, drawing a smile from the man.

"Doesn't matter. You're coming with us. Between the two of you, you're a cool fifteen mil for me and my boys. Pretty good pay for a half-day's work, if I say so myself." He pulled out a pair of handcuffs and dangled them from one finger. "No funny business now. Oh yeah, and there was something about a lizard…"

Penny poked her head over Finn's shoulder, baring her teeth.

The man took a backwards step. "The fuck is that thing?"

"Armor?" Finn asked Mila.

"On," she replied.

"Do it, Penny!" While the merc commander was blocking his men's line of fire, Finn dropped his hand and grabbed Fragar.

Penny opened her maw and blasted the man with drag-onfire, then launched at the closest merc on the right, spreading her wings and sending another jet of fire.

The commander beat at the magical flames. He spun and sprinted for a snowdrift, then dove into it, sending up a gout of steam as the flames flash-boiled the snow. The rest of the mercs hesitated. Half of them went to help their commander. The others were faltered by the impossibility that an actual dragon had set two of them on fire.

A loud *thump* resounded from Finn's right. A net fired from a cannon-like gun wrapped around Penny in midflight and sparked with electricity. The little dragon hit the snowy ground in a tangled heap, out cold.

That was it. These fools were going to die.

Fragar held high, Finn bellowed and charged.

CHAPTER TWENTY-TWO

Penny's unconscious body was wrapped in a net pulsing with electricity. A merc with a remote turned off the shocking feature and approached to retrieve the dragon.

Mila willed her panic away. She was the only one of them who could take a bullet, provided it hit her torso. She reached into her coat for the Ivar pistol and pulled the weapon out, praying she had the power to use it. Targeting the merc stooping by Penny, she pulled the trigger just as those aiming at Finn unleashed a barrage. The roar of seven rifles all but deafened her, although it wasn't nearly as deafening as the silence from the Ivar. The gun didn't even hiccup.

Bullets ricocheted around Finn, and the dwarf blocked one with the flat of Fragar, then he was on the first man. The axe came down and sliced the merc's automatic rifle in half. The soldier stumbled backward.

Mila stuffed her useless weapon into its holster and

pulled Gram out. She whispered the power word to extend the golden blade.

A merc coming her way stopped when he saw the blade unfurl. Mila leapt at him, swinging the sword for all her worth. The man raised his gun to block the blade.

Mila used the momentum of the deflection and spun into a reverse heel kick. Her heel slammed into the side of his head, catching him on the cheek, and he flopped to the ground.

Mila almost pumped her fist. She had actually done it! She wanted to scream with joy, but a second merc hit her from the side, and they both struck the ground. Gram skittered into the snow as air vacated her lungs. She saw spots, then she felt her arms wrenched behind her. In the time it took for her to coax air back into her lungs, she was hauled to her feet with her hands ziptied behind her.

---

Finn's rage gripped hold of him as Fragar's razor edge took the merc's leg clean off. The man missed the chance to scream, as Finn removed his head with a backswing. That was two down in a matter of seconds.

A rifle butt slammed into his face, and Finn went to one knee. A second blow to the back of his head made him go down on his left hand. The pain didn't register, just a dull *thump* in the back of his perception, yet the angle afforded him a view of Mila being hauled up, her hands tied behind her back.

Finn saw red.

He tried to summon his magic, but the rage kept it out of reach.

A third blow struck his shoulder. Finn ignored it. He began taking deep, slow breaths.

The men continued hammering at him, but Finn's internal war took his entire focus. He slowed his heart and let his mind calm despite his boiling blood. The rage started to change, and then his body changed. He focused on his breath. Somehow he knew it wasn't enough.

Not knowing what to do, he spoke to the rage directly. *You are mine. I am not controlled by you. You bow to* my *authority. You will conform.*

A second or two passed. His heart kept slowing, but his power remained. His mind cleared, yet retained its savage edge.

Finn opened his eyes and focused on the ground behind Mila. He manifested his will into form. Moments ago, his magic was out of reach. His mind stretched for it, rebelling at the very concept of using magic while in a rage.

He pushed through. *"Colún cloiche. Coinnigh í"* he roared with a war cry, his fist slamming the snowy earth.

An earth and granite pillar erupted from the ground beneath the merc who'd been forcing Mila toward the helicopter. It arose with such speed, it punched him into the air, tearing free his grasp on Mila.

The man catapulted forty feet into the air. The mercs stopped pounding on Finn and observed their screaming comrade fly over the side of the precipice.

Finn struck the merc in front of him with an uppercut from Fragar. The blade passed through the man's forearm, and the merc stared incredulously at the stump of his arm as it geysered blood. He then screamed and drew the rest of his comrades' attentions back to Finn.

———

The earth shook a split second before the ground shot upward behind Mila and took her captor with it. Considering how tight the man gripped the shoulder of her coat, she thought she was going with him into the air. To her surprise, she felt her feet lock into a pair of stone arches that had formed at the same time as the erupting column.

His hold on her wrenched free by his own momentum, the merc arced over the edge of the cliff. Her heart pounded as she assessed the situation and stepped out of the stone loops.

She observed Finn slice the arm off one of his attackers. Then she headed straight for the man holding the net with Penny tangled in it. He was aiming a pistol at Finn's back. Mila caught Penny's eye, surprised the tiny dragon had come to so fast. Penny winked and sucked in a breath.

The sound alerted the merc. Rather than pull the trigger, he glanced at Penny, who unleashed a stream of dragonfire across his arm and face. He screamed and flailed, backpedaling and trying to put the flames out.

Mila body-checked him from behind, and they all tumbled to the ground. He was preoccupied with the flames and didn't pay her any heed. Penny had come loose, and Mila rolled away and maneuvered her arms to snatch Penny up while still ziptied and the dragon still inside the net. Thankfully, the dragon was light.

Mila bolted for the car while one of Penny's claws

poked out of the net and sawed through the zipties. Her hands suddenly and unexpectedly free, Mila stumbled but regained her balance. She knelt and started to unwrap the dragon, who writhed with the need to get back into the fight.

"Stop moving! I can't get this loose if you keep going crazy!"

The dragon calmed, and Mila took the last loop free. The net fell away in a tangled mess. Penny shot straight up into the air and soared for Finn. Mila saw the two remaining mercs, one of whom lacked an arm, leap into the Black Hawk as it lifted, then slid over the open air and beyond the cliff.

Mila gazed around and did a quick count. Six bodies. Well, six and an eighth, after she included the severed arm at Finn's feet.

She fell onto her butt and brushed wet hair away from her face. "What the hell was that?" she said to herself.

## CHAPTER TWENTY-THREE

Despite the rage boiling in his core, for the first time, Finn was thinking clearly as it flowed through him. He watched the Black Hawk descend into the clouds, the *whump-whump* of its rotor fading. For a few seconds, there was no sound whatsoever, and he took a deep breath to release the rage. It lumbered deep into his body like a bear off to hibernate in its cave.

A sensation of letting go, rather than having escaped the bear's clutches, felt refreshing, even liberating.

Penny landed on his shoulder and placed her small clawed hand on his temple. She pulled it back in surprise when she didn't sense his post-battle frenzy. The dragon cocked her head at him. "Shir?"

He smiled. "I tried Rolf's breathing technique. I think I might keep that up."

She raised an eye ridge.

Finn laughed. "I'll tell you later." He spotted Mila sitting in the snow and rushed to her side. "Are you okay? Did my magic hurt you?"

She shook her head and returned to the present. "No, that was awesome. Ripped the guy right off me, then I was able to get Penny free." She glanced around the carnage and back at him. "Considering this fucking mess, hell, I'm shipshape."

He took her hand and helped her to her feet. She wiped wet snow from her butt and legs and marched toward a snow bank.

"What are you doing?" Finn asked her.

"Getting Gram. I dropped it in the fight." She knelt and rummaged in the snow until she pulled her hand out, Gram in her grip. She whispered the power word, and the sword folded into the handle. She stowed it at the small of her back and smiled woodenly at Finn. "Ready."

He gripped her shoulders and made her look at him. "You're scaring me, Mila. Are you sure you weren't hurt?"

She deflated in his grip and sighed. "I guess that was just *really* close. The other times, we've had a pretty easy way of it, but a fucking military chopper full of fucking trained soldiers? The only reason we got out of this is because they had no idea about magic. What if next time a trained group of Kashgar come after us instead of humans? I'm no use to you guys. I'm a liability."

He shook his head. "Where is this all coming from?"

She pulled out the Ivar pistol. "I tried to use it. Nothing. Then I went after them with Gram, and they took me down after the first swing."

Finn grabbed the gun and examined it while Penny hopped onto Mila's shoulder and began rubbing the top of her head and cooing.

"Two things. First, you freed Penny during the fight.

Nobody did that but you. And that's a hell of a lot more than nothing. We owe you."

Mila shook her head. "The fight was over by the time I got her free."

"You didn't know that. If one of those guys had taken me down with their initial barrage, it would have made a huge difference." He waved a hand back and forth. "It doesn't matter how this turned out, you fought and freed your comrade during that fight. We should all have that kind of bravery and tenacity."

Mila *harrumphed* and crossed her arms, but she didn't argue. "What's the second thing?"

He handed her the pistol and pointed to a switch on the back. "You had the safety on."

She stared at the gun, then glared at him. "You didn't tell me it has a safety."

He shrugged. "Honestly, I didn't know until I looked." He perked up at the distant sound of sirens and glanced toward the road. It was clear of cars, but that wouldn't last. "We need to get out of here. You good to drive?"

Knowing the gun didn't fire because of a technical issue rather than her lack of magic, Mila brightened. She reached around and clicked the Ivar into its holster. "Yeah, we don't want to be anywhere near here."

"You get enough stretching in?" Finn asked with a smile as he opened the car door for her.

Mila rolled her eyes. "Not only did I stretch, I got a workout in, too."

Finn watched the road ahead for flashing lights. Three oncoming SUVs labeled State Highway Patrol moved at a pretty good clip considering the conditions, heading toward the pulloff battleground they'd left behind. He didn't envy them. After the shock wore off, he wondered how their paperwork would explain finding six-and-an-eighth well-armed mercenaries sprawled dead in red-stained snow.

On the next switchback, they passed over top of the Berthound Pass Trailhead pulloff. Looking down, Finn saw dozens of flashing lights and several patrol cars.

They continued up the mountain in silence until Finn pulled out a box of Charleston Chews and shook a few into his hand. He offered the box to Mila, who shook her head. "I can't eat yet. I'm still too worked up."

"I get it. That was some shit." He handed what was left to Penny.

"They're going to keep coming, aren't they?" Mila asked him.

Finn nodded. "And they're going to get better and be better equipped, too, as the price goes up. I tried to get Hellena to drop it, but she's determined."

Mila peered at him, confusion on her face. "Hellena? Who's that?"

"The Dark Star. Her name's Hellena." He fidgeted upon realizing he hadn't told her about the call. Things *had* been busy after all.

"And how do you know that? Isn't her identity some big secret or something?"

Finn gave her a weak smile. "She called my phone this morning."

Mila blinked at him, looked back at the road, and blinked again. "She called you? She has your number? That doesn't worry you?"

"I mean, it wasn't the highlight of my day."

"Oh, really? What trumps getting a call from the woman trying to kill us as the highlight of your day?"

Finn thought about that as he tossed another chew in his mouth. "To be honest, so far the highlight was getting to watch you stretch when we got out of the car. You know, before the attack."

They passed a slow-moving car, and Finn watched Mila, worried what she would say next. He was joking about the stretching thing, but he should have told her about the call. To be honest, he didn't know why he hadn't. That wasn't true. He didn't want to tell her Hellena put a bounty on his friends as motivation for him to join her.

Suddenly, Mila laughed. "Watching me stretch was more impressive than a call from the Dark Star." She gave him a sidelong grin. "Hey, I work hard for this caboose, man."

"And it's appreciated. In general, I mean. I don't think you keep it," he waved a hand around vaguely, "tight, for my sake." He put his head in his hand and sighed. "Why is talking to you so hard?"

Penny perched in between them, grinning like she was enjoying her favorite soap opera. She reached into the box of Chews without taking her eyes off them.

Mila chuckled and patted Finn's knee while she kept her eyes on the road. "It's fine. We ripped the dating Band-Aid off last night, and now the wound is a little raw." She considered that, then added, "Of course, maybe analogizing our relationship to a wound isn't the best choice."

He snorted, then said, "Sorry I didn't tell you. About the call. She made some threats about you and pretty much everyone around me, and I didn't want to scare you. You have enough to deal with."

"Oh, please. She can't threaten us anymore than she has already. I mean, there's a pretty hefty bounty on my head already. Speaking of, how do we get rid of those? I *would* like to be able to walk down the street again someday."

Finn puffed out his cheeks and exhaled. "Either get her to take it down or make her take it down." He nodded, thinking it through. "Or, you know, we can kill her. If there's no one to ante up, there's no more bounty hunters."

She frowned. "Was that, like, an apple-a-day pun?"

"A what?"

"Never mind." Mila shook her head, a smile on her face. "I wonder if those guys are going to report back to the Dark...Hellena. If so, it could mean trouble if she knows we're heading to the lake. Maybe we should let Danica know to watch out for trouble."

"Danica is in the safest place in Colorado right now. Well, maybe the safest private residence. Actually, the second safest private—"

"I get it. The cabin is warded to hell and back. That's all fine and dandy, but it only keeps her safe if she stays indoors."

"She teleported up. No one knows she's there. She'll be fine. Besides, we told her not to go out." Finn fetched a can of Pringles from the plastic bag with all their road trip supplies. "Now, let's see what all the fuss is with these stackable chips."

"Five bucks says you get ten chips in then rip the can in half. No way you're getting those big fingers in there without crushing 'em."

"I'll have you know I have slender fingers." He waggled them in front of his face.

Mila raised both eyebrows. "You call those slender? I've eaten hotdogs daintier than those things."

"Well, they're slender for a dwarf," he said before reaching into the can and crushing the top chip. "Ah, fuck."

Penny laughed and nearly choked on a Chew.

# CHAPTER TWENTY-FOUR

The Hellcat rumbled to a stop at the first intersection off the highway that led into the town of Grand Lake, presenting a distant view of the idyllic snow-covered buildings lining Main Street.

Mila leaned on the steering wheel and scanned the street. "Not many people around."

"It's pretty cold out. Maybe they're all inside."

She shook her head. "I doubt it. This place is usually packed with people coming up for ice fishing. The lake froze over more than a month ago, but I don't see all that many huts out there." She pointed where the land sloped to a frozen lake surrounded by white mountains. Finn could pick out small huts and tents dotting the frozen surface, but it wasn't crowded by any means. "Plus, there's cabins and the nearby hot springs that bring in vacationers as soon as the snow starts falling." She bit her lip, tapping the gas to roll into town proper. "Something's off. Do you feel, like, a heaviness in the air?"

Finn cocked an eyebrow. Now that she pointed it out,

he did feel something magical in nature going on. If Mila felt it too, that meant she was connecting to her peabrain for sure. Even if it was a tiny bit, he was happy to know the circlet hadn't burned her out.

Penny climbed up from Finn's lap onto the dashboard and checked things out with a wary eye. She was far more sensitive to magic than either of them. Unlike most magicals, dragons were sensitive enough to pick out what spell was being used half the time.

The magical pressure grew as they got closer to town. By the time they approached a large wooden sign that read Welcome to Grand Lake, Finn's brain ached. Mila rolled past the sign and, suddenly, the pressure vanished.

"Uh...what happened?" Mila looked around. "The feeling of dread just...disappeared."

"Squee krii. Shir, chi chi," Penny said.

"She says a spell is covering the entire town," Finn translated.

"Is that a big deal? From the looks on your faces, that's a big deal."

"It's a big deal. A continuous spell of this magnitude requires a tremendous amount of power. An unbelievable amount."

Mila's face showed signs of worry. "Are we in trouble here?"

Finn shook his head. "We're okay. The spell is meant to keep people away. To a nonmagical, the sense of dread would be so potent most people would turn around." He glanced at Mila. "I guess we know why there aren't a lot of people here. It looks like the Dark Star is driving them away."

They rolled through the main drag and headed toward the road that circled around the lake. Even in the heart of town, they only spied the occasional person, and most of them had the look of locals.

"Is there a military base around here?" Finn asked.

"No. I don't think so. Why?" Mila was reading the names of the shops.

Finn pointed to a pair of black, military-style Humvees parked on the street in front of a building with a sign that read The Worlds End Brewpub and Inn.

"Those look like private military," Mila said.

Finn sighed, rubbing a hand over his face. "Looks like Hellena has this place locked down more than we thought."

"What does that mean for us?" Mila turned off the main drag, which Finn noticed was fittingly called Grand Avenue.

"It means she's not fucking around with the *Anthem*. I was hoping we could disable the ship and come back for it later. If she's putting these kinds of resources into it, there is no way she'll consider slinking away with her tail between her legs." He gave Penny a serious look. "We may have to blow the ship up. We can't let her get it running, and I don't see how we can steal it back."

Penny frowned but nodded. "Chi."

Finn watched the smoke ring rising from her nostril and held out a fist for her to bump. "What the hell, right? It's not like we were ever going to leave here, were we?"

Penny smiled and bumped his fist.

Everything from little shacks to sprawling mansions lined the winding road circling the lake. Every one wanted a piece of the lake for themselves and squeezed in wherever they could. Many of the homes were empty vacation getaways, but a few had lights on and smoke coming out of the chimneys.

Finn saw why the area drew so many people. It was stunning. The tall mountain peaks and forest surrounded them in every direction with the pristine glacial lake at the center. He would like to come back in the summer to see how it looked without a fluffy layer of snow hiding much of it.

"This is it," Mila said, checking the map on her phone one last time before pulling into the snowy, evergreen-lined drive.

The tall, dense pines blocked all views of the cabin. Finn chuckled when they came around the driveway's tight S-curve. "This is a cabin? It's bigger than I thought it would be."

Mila laughed. "Only one of the richest men in the world would call this a cabin. This is a straight-up mansion. Sure, it's made of logs, but that's the only similarity I can see."

Finn's pocket warmed, and he pulled out the metal card Preston had given him. Runes glowed deep in the metal. It sent out a pulse of energy, then the card returned to its previous state of looking like a mundane, metal keycard.

"Well, I guess this is the right place." He stuffed the card back into his pocket and squinted out the window at the towering home.

They climbed out and the biting cold hit them like a

hammer. Over the last few miles, they had risen a few thousand feet, and it was evident in the temperature.

"Oh, fuck! I should have brought another jacket." Mila threw on her now-dirty white coat.

"You don't like that one?"

She shook her head. "No, it's fine. I meant *another* coat to put over this one."

Finn chuckled and went around to the trunk for their bags. "Well, let's get inside and see if Danica and the twins have a fire going."

Mila rubbed her hands together. "Good idea. You need any help?"

"I've got it. You keep those hands in your pockets. I don't want them freezing off before we can get anything done."

"Ha!" She gave him the finger and stuffed her hands in her pockets. "You don't know what it's like to be small in the cold. Goes right to the bone." She shivered to emphasize her point.

They followed a winding path around to the side of the house, cleared of snow and ice either by Danica or more magical means woven into the house, which wouldn't surprise them. A row of pines blocked their view of the side, but they came to the end of it where the path turned and gave them a sweeping view of the lake with no houses or buildings to be seen anywhere.

"Holy shit, that's beautiful," Mila said from deep in her hood.

The house sat on the bank, and a long dock stretched out onto the frozen water. The wind blew the snow on the lake into drifts as tall as Finn in some places, leaving the dark blue ice exposed in others.

"Who the fuck are you?"

Finn and Mila turned and saw Danica standing on a second-story balcony that wrapped around the house, her white hood up and her bow nocked with an arrow and pointed at them. As soon as they looked her way, she lowered the weapon with a breath of relief.

"Oh, shit. I didn't expect you two for hours with how bad the roads are. I thought you may have been bounty hunters. Sorry!" She replaced the arrow into the quiver on her hip, then waved them up a set of stairs. "Come in through here. I still have warm cocoa on the stove."

Finn followed Mila up the steps, lifting the three bags over the rails so he could ascend the narrow stairway.

The huge balcony extended from the main living area of the house. The floor-to-ceiling window wall could fold to expose the interior to the elements in warmer months, with doors built into the glass for cooler days. Finn spotted a massive hot tub at the corner of the balcony that could fit a dozen people. Beside it, a heated lap pool gave off wisps of steam in the frosty air. They also discerned a stone fireplace surrounded by benches and tables and outdoor heaters.

"Classy place," Finn commented to Penny, perching on his shoulder.

"Chi shir." It took a lot to impress her, but this place was doing it.

They entered the 'cabin' via the glass doors. Finn dropped the bags and grabbed for Fragar at the sound of gunfire.

"Don't mind them, they've been playing since we got here," Danica said with an eye roll, hiking a thumb to the enormous TV on the wall above a fireplace. "Guys, it's so loud you almost got Fragar'd!"

Finn smiled. He liked that term.

The twins waved as they played a game that entailed shooting each other and everyone else around them.

"Hey, Ronan. Regan. How are you two doing?" Finn called out over the sound of artificial machine gun fire.

In unison, they said, "Hey'a. Good."

"They haven't left the couch since we got here," Danica told him. "Luckily, there's a second living room downstairs."

Mila took off her coat and laid it on the giant butcher block counter that covered a huge kitchen island, then began to rummage in the cupboards until she found mugs and pulled three of them out. "You two want cocoa?"

Finn and Penny nodded.

"Sure. What's cocoa?" Finn asked, moving the duffel bags to a second couch that faced the glass wall.

Mila froze and cocked her head. "You've never had cocoa?"

He and Penny shook their heads. "No. But I like the name."

She smiled. "Oh, man. You two are gonna lose your minds. It'll satisfy even your sweet tooth."

"It's sweet? I'm in."

She ladled three mugs full from the steaming pot on the stove and set two of them on the island before inhaling the steam from her own cup and taking a sip.

Finn picked up his mug and Penny hopped down to the

counter to sniff at hers. They glanced at one another, eyes wide with excitement from the chocolaty scent.

Finn tilted the mug back and took a big gulp of the nearly-boiling liquid, swishing it around in his mouth a few times before swallowing. He smiled and took another gulp.

"Slow down, big guy," Danica said, horror on her face. "Sip it. Make it last longer. We only have so much."

"It's like a melted chocolate bar," he said before taking a smaller gulp.

Mila laughed. "Finally found a hot drink he won't put those damned Chews into."

Finn reached into his pocket and pulled out a box. "You're right, I should try that." He dumped a few of the little chocolate-covered nougats into the cocoa.

"You have got to be kidding me," Mila said, but she handed him a spoon anyway.

"Thanks." Finn stirred the drink and, when he figured the candies were good and melted, took an exploratory sip, once again swishing the liquid back and forth in his mouth. He smiled at Mila. "You were right. Even better."

"How do you even have teeth left?"

He shrugged. "Good bones."

# CHAPTER TWENTY-FIVE

Danica, Mila, and Penny joined Finn on the balcony to put some distance between them and the sounds of the video game. The ladies shivered after only a minute, so Finn fired up one of the tall outdoor heaters.

"You said there were hunters snooping around? Were they on the property?" Finn sat in a teak armchair, putting his second mug of cocoa and Chews on the table.

"No, I saw them in town when I went for groceries. I guess even the rich and powerful don't keep the refrigerator stocked when they're not around."

Mila frowned at her friend. "Finn said not to leave the house."

Danica gave a helpless shrug. "What was I supposed to do? Six mouths to feed and no food? I figured I should go before you three got here and started kicking the hornets' nest."

Mila huffed, knowing Danica was right. "I suppose. No one knows to look for you up here, but after the attack on the highway, I'm sure they'll be all over us."

They had told Danica about the attack in the kitchen, before the sounds of gunfire became too distracting, and they ventured outside.

"I can't believe they sent a helicopter after you." Danica shook her head in disbelief. "I can hardly get people to call me back about their test results, and you have people hunting you down in Black Hawks."

"I'm not convinced the guys in that helicopter are the same organization as the ones here," Finn said, unable to resist another large gulp before continuing. "It didn't have any markings and was the same matte black as the Humvees, but not as new. Looked like it was fifty years old."

Penny shook her head and frowned. "Shir chi? Squee shir."

"I know it's flimsy, but that was only the first part." Finn continued his theory. "The real reason I don't think they're the same organization is those guys might have been seasoned soldiers, yet they nearly lost it when we started using magic."

"What does that have to do with it?" Danica asked.

"The Dark Star wouldn't recruit clueless mundanes to her personal army. Makes no sense."

Penny gave him a bow along with a golf clap.

He glared at her. "Ass."

She snickered, then took a drink of her cocoa and gazed at the lake. "Shee chir?"

"Yeah, scouting's a good idea, but stay away from anyone you spot out there. Remember, Hellena is probably up here somewhere, and if she's powerful enough to keep a spell over an entire town, she'll know if you do anything flashy."

"Wait," Danica held up a hand, stalling Penny. "When I was at the checkout, the clerk told me the mercenaries had come to town about a month ago. I asked why the sheriff hadn't kicked them out. He said they had all the proper licenses and stuff, so there wasn't anything he could do." She pointed to the south side of the lake to their right. "He said there's some big VIP at a house on the south shore. It's got to be her."

Penny smiled, gave her a thumbs-up, and flew to the door. Using magic, she slid the door open and went to her bag, zipped it open, and crawled inside.

Finn and the women exchanged glances.

Penny popped out of the bag, holding a pair of expensive binoculars. She trotted out and handed them to Finn.

"State of the art stuff here," he said, looking them over. On the side was a switch for night vision, along with a ridiculous zoom feature and a built-in camera. Unlike normal binoculars with double-tube optics, these were boxy with three lenses on one side and a rubber cup shaped like a face mask on the other.

"Where the hell did you get these?"

"Shir shee. Chi chi."

"Ah, Grace." He held the binoculars up. "Why not order them online or whatever you do?"

Penny told him you can't buy stuff like that if you're a civilian. You need to know people, or know people that know people. Or be government. Turns out Grace was someone who knows people; either that, or she convinced someone she worked for the CIA.

"Let me get this straight. You found an assistant online. Hired her, then one of the first things you did was have her buy military-grade hardware and, not only did she get it done, but she didn't even ask questions?"

Penny puffed a smoke ring out of one nostril without breaking eye contact.

Finn blew out a breath. "Well, shit. She really is the best assistant in the world."

Another smoke ring.

"Okay, okay. No need to say I told you so."

Penny smiled and lazily saluted. She started toward the end of the table, then turned back, gulped the rest of her cocoa, turned again and, after a running start, zipped into the air. She was lost in the brilliant afternoon sun within seconds.

Mila's stomach growled loud enough to be heard.

Finn peered at her. "I could eat too."

Mila rolled her eyes as Danica got up. "Good thing I hit up the grocery then. I have lunch all ready. I'll go grab it." She headed inside.

"Bring the twins back, too. We need to put together a game plan," Finn called after her, and she waved in acknowledgment.

***

Everyone chattered and ate their meatball sandwiches while Finn leaned against the railing, trying to figure out how to use the damn space binoculars. Every time he went to zoom, the focus went fuzzy. When he 'reverse-zoomed,' he couldn't find anything. He eventually left the zoom all the way out and figured out how to get the image in focus, then he aimed in the general direction of the south shore and scanned each house.

He spent several minutes getting motion sickness because he couldn't keep the stupid binoculars steady enough.

Mila appeared at the railing beside him and held out a plate with a sandwich and chips on it. "Better eat this before it freezes into a meatball ice block. So, what's the plan?"

"Well, that's what we have to decide." He set the binoculars down and accepted the plate.

Penny was still out scouting, so she wasn't there to eat his unattended food, like she was prone to do. He called over to the table. "Regan, what do you two need to get down there? Can we bust a hole in the ice at the shoreline?"

The young selkie swallowed her bite and shook her head, but Ronan answered. "The shore will be too far to swim. We can shift into otters, but otters still need to breathe. If we're going to get down there and look around, or whatever you need us to do, we'll need the shortest route."

"I was afraid you'd say that. So we need to get out on the ice and bust a hole in it, without being spotted."

"We could use a fishing tent." Mila pointed at the dozens on the ice.

Finn peered at the tents and small shacks on the ice. "Would it be odd to take one of those tents to the middle? Seems most are near the shore."

Mila frowned. "I'm not sure. I don't know jack about ice fishing."

"It would be a little odd on this lake," Regan said, with a shrug.

Her brother picked up the narrative. "Grand Lake is, like, four-hundred feet deep. It's not common to fish in water that deep."

"So no one does it?" Finn asked.

They looked at one another, then Regan said, "Always the odd person who does it. Ice fishing is more about drinking anyway, so if you don't care about catching much, it's the best way to get away from everyone."

Finn crossed his arms. "I suppose we'll chance it. Preston said there was scuba gear here, but the point is for you two to blend in with the environment. Going down with a tank on your back would be like a target on your forehead."

"I saw a shack thing in the boathouse when I explored the place this morning." Danica said.

Finn leaned forward to see the green metal roof of a large garage-like structure extending halfway into the lake close to the dock. "Anything in there to pull it?"

She nodded. "There's one of those four wheelers with ice chains on it."

"Well, that's sorted." Finn turned to the twins. "Now, onto to what it is I need you to do."

They straightened. "Whatever you need."

Finn and Mila joined everyone at the table. "First of all, it's a scouting mission. If you get down there and find the ship surrounded by the enemy, get straight back here. We'll figure something else out. But the main goal is getting the *Anthem's* fuel rod."

Ronan cocked his head. "Fuel rod? Like in a reactor?

Aren't those, like, inside a power plant or something? Is it in the engine room?"

Finn shook his head. "Ships like the *Anthem* run on pure magical energy. Theoretically, any magic user could refuel the ship if they had enough time, although the amount for that would be ridiculous. That's not the point. The point is when you refuel your ship, instead of having a bunch of people channeling power into it, they simply swap the empty fuel rod with one already charged."

"Then why can't she just replace the rod if we take it?" Mila asked.

"A vessel made to hold the kinds of power I'm talking about isn't made from common materials by some craftsman down on the corner. Fuel rods are dwarven and made with secret techniques my family won't share with anyone. That's why dwarves rule the universe. Without them, no fuel rods."

"Wait," Danica said. "You're saying your father makes all these, and thats why he's the king?"

"Well, he doesn't make them personally, but yeah. It's the family business."

Regan steered them back on track. "So, how do we get this thing out?"

Finn smiled, and took a small metal disk from his pocket. "With this. It's a docking chit. I had to hand it over to the dockmaster when we stopped at a station so they could get to the maintenance sections. If you have this, you hit the eject button for the rod, and it slides right out."

"And where is that?" Ronan asked, raising an eyebrow. "Isn't the ship an asteroid? How can we tell the front from the back?"

"Well, that's the tricky part." Finn pulled a pen and small pad of paper from his jacket pocket.

"What else you got in those pockets, big guy?" Mila asked with a half-smile.

He grinned and began sketching a rough of the *Anthem's* layout.

"That's a drawing of a circle," Ronan said.

Finn glanced up. "I said it would be tricky."

# CHAPTER TWENTY-SIX

After thirty minutes, the twins were confident they could find the fuel rod port at the back of the *Anthem*, although Finn's crude sketch was little help. Ronan and Regan went inside to change clothes. They needed to wear something they could get in and out of quickly for their shifting.

Finn raised the last bite of his cold meatball sandwich when Penny landed on the table and crossed her arms, eying his last bite. He looked her in the eyes and stuffed it in his mouth. She returned a narrow gaze.

Mila held out the last sandwich. "Don't worry. We didn't forget about you, Penny."

Penny took it and gave Mila a smile before tearing the foil wrapping and diving into the marinara-soaked bun.

"What did you find?" Finn asked.

"Shi chi shir?" The tiny dragon pointed at her sandwich.

He chuckled. "Okay then, I'll fill you in on what we came up with."

He laid out the idea to take the fuel rod to disable the

CHARLEY CASE

ship. Penny made a few suggestions between bites, and
Finn made notes in his head, refining what he would tell
the twins when they returned.

"That still leaves the question of how I get on board to
destroy it. Dwarves are not very good in water." Finn
frowned, trying to think of the best way to get down there,
and coming up with nothing but the scuba gear.

"Why do you need to get on board?" Danica asked.
"Can't you strap explosives to it or something?"

He shook his head. "It's too big for that. We would need
tons of explosives to crack the *Anthem's* hull. I need to get
on board so I can engage the self-destruct mechanism...
though that would be a pretty big bang that I don't know if
we can all get clear of in time."

"Squee shir shee krii." Penny took her last bite and
patted her belly.

Finn frowned, but nodded. "I don't like it, but it's an
option. As long as you're certain the lake could absorb the
blast."

"The blast?" Mila asked.

"Penny suggested we use the fuel rod to blow up the
*Anthem*. She could set it to overload and drop it in the
water over the ship. That would take care of it."

Mila shook her head. "No way. There's a town over
there full of people. If you blow up the *Anthem*, it might kill
everyone around here. You may as well use the self
destruct. I saw how massive an explosion the Huldu used
the first time. A blast that big would blow all the water out
of the lake."

"It wouldn't be like that," Finn assured her. "What the

186

Huldu did was use magic to create an explosion. This is different, an explosion of magical energy."

Mila looked around the table with a blank stare. "How's that different?"

Danica put her elbows on the table. "Rupturing a magical item works in a similar way to, like, a regular explosion, releasing a lot of power very quickly and, if it happened on the surface, the magical explosion would be just as devastating, like when the Dark Star threatened to rupture the Helm of Awe. But because it would happen underwater, that changes things."

Finn nodded and picked up the explanation. "Magic has a lot of interesting properties, but one of the most interesting is how it interacts with water when in its raw form. Casting underwater is not a problem since you never release raw magic; you first form it into whatever spell you want, then release it. But when it's raw, it wants to find equilibrium, and water is a nearly perfect environment. So, the water absorbs the raw magic it encounters, kind of like radiation."

"Okay..." Mila followed so far. "What happens if you rupture the rod deep in the water?"

"It would warp everything in the vicinity to unusable scrap. The *Anthem* would crumble to dust, and everything on board would fuse into a lump of inert material. There would be an explosion, since the water can only absorb so much, but the lake is deep, and Penny thinks it wouldn't make much difference on the surface."

Mila turned to Penny, who nodded.

"Okay, Finn, so why don't you like the idea?"

"Overloading a fuel rod isn't like putting a timer on a

bomb." He sighed. "It's more like lighting a fuse, but you don't know how long the fuse is. It could take two seconds or two hours to blow. I'm concerned it would be on the two-second side of things, which is a less desirable outcome, since the magic needs time to build pressure enough to rupture the rod." He frowned, considering the idea further before shaking his head. "It's something we can decide later. We'll have the twins get a quick look first. I don't want them taking any chances, so scouting mission first, then decide what to do." He held up the high-tech binoculars to Penny. "Can you show me how to use these damned things? I can't get them to focus or zoom right."

Penny examined them and flipped a small switch on top. The binoculars made a quiet humming noise that increased in tone until Finn couldn't hear it anymore, like a capacitor had powered up.

"Oh. I didn't realize there was an electronic element to them."

Penny smiled, and patted his hand in a motherly fashion. "Chi chi."

"Like a safety switch," Mila grinned at him.

"Shut up. Both of you." He laughed. "Pen, this is why you're in charge of the gadgets."

Finn used the binoculars, without wanting to puke his meatball sub, and scanned the south shore with Penny pointing out the house. He found the place. It was nearly as big and luxurious as Preston's place. Unlike Preston's cabin, though, it was stone and sported large Gothic style windows and trim. It reminded him of a castle, but more modern.

As he scanned the large balcony—with its own hot tub and pool, of course—Penny informed him what she'd seen. A half-dozen Humvees parked out front along with a few dozen snowmobiles. Ten to twelve guards outside, and more movement through the windows.

"Magical barrier?" Finn asked, spotting the first guard.

Penny said a few, but she couldn't tell from a distance what they did.

Finn studied the guard pacing the balcony, an automatic rifle slung across his chest, dressed in a mid-thigh white coat that hid any other weaponry. The man's features were indicative of a Kashgar, but without feeling his aura it was impossible to tell.

"I think that's a different group than the ones on the highway," Finn said, lowering the binoculars. "They look like Kashgar to me. We should be ready for magical attacks if it comes to a fight."

"Chi."

Finn sucked in a breath and considered their next move. "Are the girls getting changed?"

Penny nodded.

"Okay. I say we go soon. I think it would be odd for us to be going out on the lake too late in the afternoon. We'll already be the odd ones venturing out over the deep, but there's no helping it."

He held up the binoculars again and zoomed out to get a full-view of the house. He spotted four more guards outfitted like the one on the deck, keeping a sharp eye out. Another two guards came up the steps at the side of the house, one of them speaking into a walkie talkie. The six guards did a full sweep with eagle eyes, and Finn worried they'd gotten wind of him being in the area.

He thought about calling the whole thing off when he spied a large door open and a woman with long black hair and wearing a thin black robe step out. She had a towel around her neck and walked on bare feet through the thin layer of snow toward the hot tub.

Finn zoomed in. It surprised him how young she looked. He had expected a woman starting her own county to be, well, older. Then again, because she looked like a Peabrain didn't mean she was one. Plenty of races aged slow and looked human.

She dropped the robe to reveal pale skin and a shapely figure under her one-piece black swimsuit. She slipped into the water and leaned back, closing her eyes. It took a second before Finn noticed it, a thin haze of shadow like dark smoke shrouded her. A faint roiling cloud of dark energy, like an aura. Damn. She was powerful. It already impressed him how she could teleport something as large as an asteroid.

Finn lowered the binoculars. "She's there. Hellena. She's right fucking there."

Penny held out her hands and Finn handed the device over. The dragon did the best she could to hold the binoculars, but ended up having to rest them on a railing post and look through a single eyehole. After a few seconds, she pulled her face from the rubber pad and whistled.

"Yeah. Did you see the black smoke? Probably how she got her name."

Penny nodded.

"Change of plans," Finn said, leaning on the rail. "Only me and the twins are going out on the ice."

Penny started to protest, but Finn held up a hand. "No arguing. We weren't a hundred percent sure she was here. Now we know. I don't want all of us to be out there if we don't have to. Besides, out on the ice, we'll stick out like sore thumbs, so having a dragon with me is a dead give-away. Me and the twins look like a father and his kids going out for some fun. If we bring the whole gang, well, you get the picture. There's also the added benefit that if I get taken out, you and the girls still have a chance to deal with the *Anthem*."

Penny gave him a hard stare, her hands on her hips, but Finn could tell she agreed with his logic, even if it pissed her off. Eventually, she nodded agreement.

"Great. Let's break it to Mila and Danica." He clapped his hands together. "This ought to be fun."

"Shir shi?" Penny hopped on his shoulder as he headed toward the door.

"It's a joke, Penny. Mila's gonna blow a gasket."

# CHAPTER TWENTY-SEVEN

Mila watched from the boathouse's open garage door as Finn set off on the four-wheeler, pulling a nice fishing shack outfitted with sled rails. The chains on the ATV's tires spit up ice chips, and the twins were packed into the shed along with all the equipment they would need for their scouting mission. Mila felt confident in their abilities to blend in and hoped they would be safe.

She smiled at the thought of being able to shapeshift into an otter. She wondered if their odd human behaviorisms were because of their otter side. She giggled at the unintentional pun and her in-ear comm crackled to life.

"What's so funny?" Finn asked, the wind a lot less pronounced through his comm than she would have guessed.

"Nothing. I was thinking about Regan and Ronan's 'otter half.'" She giggled again, unable to help herself.

The twins cut in and said in unison, "Heard it a million times. Do better."

Mila laughed again.

The comms were another of Penny's mystery purchases with the company debit card. It turned out over the last few months the little dragon had collected many goodies. When she had opened the bag and shown them what was in there, it took a good fifteen minutes to go through it all. Along with the in-ear comms were military-grade tablets with everything from GPS to direct satellite data up-links on them. Body armor made from some spider-goat hybrid silk. The very idea of a goat in some lab genetically spliced with a spider to produce silk creeped Mila out, but the armor was sweet. Penny even had one made to fit Finn, and he wore it under a thick, green winter coat they'd found in the closet. They'd convinced him hitting the ice in his stitched bomber jacket would look suspicious since the temp was in the teens.

Other things in the bag included foldable batons, various tasers, and a plethora of non-lethal, but effective sprays; the only one she had heard of was mace, but one labeled Jumbo Bear Spray seemed like it would work on anything. Mila wasn't sure 'jumbo' described the can or the bear, but she figured it didn't matter to anyone who got a face full of it.

The most important thing Penny pulled from the bag was the stone skin ring Mila had worn the night they fought off Jeffery and the hellhounds. Finn gave the ring to Danica, since they knew she could power it with her magic.

He'd handed her the binoculars as well, asking her to keep watch on the Dark Star's place and to let him know if there were any changes. Mila glanced up to the balcony and saw her tall friend leaning on the railing watching the house like a hawk, her bow slung over her shoulder, a quiver of arrows on her hip.

Mila felt useless as she watched the shed slow and stop a half mile out on the ice. She saw Finn hop off and unhook the shed from the ATV. Mila wanted to be out there with them, but Finn made a good argument for her, Danica, and Penny to stay behind. She just didn't like it.

With a sigh, she headed for the door.

"You okay, Mila?" Finn asked, making her jump. She needed to get used to him being in her ear.

"Yeah. Just don't know what to do with myself right now. I don't like sitting around worrying." She stepped out of the boathouse and onto the dock, looking over and squinting in the midafternoon light at the tiny figure of Finn beside the shack as he peered her way.

"You should try the gun again. I saw a pile of frozen dirt that looked like it would make a good backstop in the sideyard."

Mila turned and saw the mound he was talking about. "Won't firing off a gun draw a bunch of attention?"

When Finn replied, she heard the muffled sound of an engine. "No. Remember the rifle Preston loaned you? Magical weapons don't make a lot of noise. Especially that one, since it doesn't fire a solid projectile. Give it a try."

Mila pulled the pistol out and cradled it in her hands. She bit her lip. "What if it doesn't work? I feel like that would be a nail in the coffin." She was quiet when she said it, but Finn had heard her.

"If it doesn't work, it doesn't mean you won't awaken. It just means it's not happening right now."

"Give it a go, Mila," Danica cut in. "Magic is a tool. We

should know if it's one you can use or not. What's the worst that could happen? By the way, Penny agrees with us. At least I think that's what she's saying."

Mila peered to see Penny gesturing at Danica. "You're right. We need to know."

"Be sure to turn the safety off," Finn joked.

"Shut up and dig that ice hole, jerk." Mila shot back, a smile on her face.

"Yes, ma'am," he replied. Before the channel cut out, the background engine sound revved up.

Mila examined the Ivar. It was sleeker than any pistol she'd used. It didn't seem to have any moving parts except for the safety switch and trigger. Where there would be writing or branding on a normal pistol, the Ivar displayed delicate scrollwork that shone silver against the black finish. It was beautiful.

*A weapon shouldn't be art*, she thought.

She lined up, facing the backstop, and aimed at the lower half of the pile so she didn't overshoot the target. Taking a deep breath, she flipped the safety and put her finger on the trigger. She gripped tight, not knowing how much kickback to expect.

Mila stood like that for a good minute, scared to pull the trigger. Not scared of the gun going off, but that it wouldn't.

"Come on, Mila. Just do it," she mumbled, too quiet for the mic in her comms to pick up.

She pulled the trigger.

Nothing happened. She pulled again. Still nothing. Flipping the safety switch the other way, she tried again. Nothing but the soft click of the trigger.

She felt a flash of shame, even though she knew it wasn't her fault.

She held the gun in the palms of her hands and frowned at it. "Why won't you work for me?"

She considered throwing the damn thing in the lake, then noticed three polished spots around the grip where her palm would lay. She glanced at her gloved hand and raised an eyebrow.

"If the magic has to come from me, maybe it has to be in contact with it, right? Maybe my glove's the problem?"

"Did you say something?" Finn shouted in her ear, the roar of the auger engine half drowning him out.

"No, it's fine," Mila responded loudly. "I'm going to try something."

"Let me know how it goes. We're about through." He cut out, leaving Mila's ears ringing.

She stripped her glove off and gripped the pistol's handle, surprised at how warm it was despite the cold. This time, when she gripped it, she thought she felt a small shock. It was slight, so she wasn't sure if it had been real or in her head.

She took aim and flipped off the safety. This time, she didn't hesitate to pull the trigger.

Pain blossomed in the back of her head as a thick white bolt of energy shot from the barrel of the gun and blasted a two-foot crater into the base of the dirt backstop. A loud *boom* echoed off the mountains, making snow fall from the shaking trees around her.

Mila fell to her knees and clutched the back of her head as an instant headache threatened to split her skull her apart.

Finn's head snapped up. The sound of an explosion echoed off the mountains and sent the thick ice beneath them vibrating.

A wave of unfamiliar power washed over him and the twins, who were already pulling their clothes off. They glanced at him, and he at them.

"What the fuck was that?" Finn yelled into the comm.

"I thought...you said the gun wouldn't hurt..." Mila croaked.

"That was the pistol? What the fuck happened?"

"Well..." she sounded like she was picking herself up off the ground. "I fired it, and it was a lot more fucking powerful than you said it would be."

"Uh, Finn?" Danica cut in, "That sent off a wave of power that hit me like a brick wall."

"We felt it all the way over here. Hey, what are the Dark Star's people doing?"

"They're in a fuss, but don't seem to be making a move so far."

"Should we go or stay?" Regan asked Finn, her shirt halfway off.

He bit his cheek then chanced another look through some less powerful binoculars Penny had given him. Danica was right, they were searching the area but not making moves toward their Humvees or snowmobiles.

He turned to the twins. "Go. We might not get another chance, so if the ship is unguarded, go for it, but if you see even one person, I don't care if they're busy doing something else, get the hell out of there. We'll figure something else out."

They nodded and tossed their clothes to the side. Regan jumped, hopping into the air above the large hole Finn had augered, her feet together and arms to her side. She shifted right before going beneath the water, a large brown and black otter slipping through the hole without even a splash.

Ronan gave Finn a salute and followed his sister, also shifting in the blink of an eye and into the freezing water just as fast.

"Oh, shit…" Danica's voice came over the comm.

"What?" Finn immediately saw what had caught her attention.

Hellena was out onto the balcony. She wore a hooded black and red cloak. She stepped to the rail, and Finn trained the binoculars on her as she slowly scanned the lake, her head swiveling. His blood froze when her gaze locked on him.

She pointed right at him, and Finn saw her guards spring to action, flooding out of the house. In seconds, dozens of snowmobiles roared around the house and onto the ice, headed his way.

"Finn…" Danica called.

"I see them."

# CHAPTER TWENTY-EIGHT

M ila climbed to her feet, head still aching, although the pain subsided with every passing second.

Penny swooped down and landed on her shoulder. "Shir chi?" The dragon placed a hand on Mila's temple, closing her eyes.

"No, I'm fine." The stabbing pain at the back of her skull was now but a dull throb. It felt like when she worked out too hard and her arms were jelly the next day. She could still use them, but they ached. It was as if her brain had done a strenuous lifting session and was speeding through the recovery.

Penny took her hand away after a few seconds and petted Mila's head affectionately.

"Thanks," Mila said, meaning it.

She turned to head up the stairs to see what was happening but stopped when Danica barreled down the steps and sprinted for the boathouse. "We have to get out there and help," she yelled over her shoulder. "He's going to be overrun, and the twins are in the water without comms! Come on, there's another four-wheeler in the boathouse."

"So much for staying behind," Mila shouted as Danica ducked through the door. Mila followed on her heels.

The open garage door gave them a clear view. The color drained from Mila's face when she saw all the snow-mobiles racing across the lake toward Finn. Danica motioned for her to drive, hopping on the back of the ATV and leaving space for Mila between her long legs.

"You drive, and I'll use my bow," she said to Mila. "Though I don't know how accurate I'll be from a moving vehicle."

Mila climbed on in front of her friend. She did a quick check and felt her gun and Gram in their holsters, along with two healing potions in their hard pockets.

She started the four-wheeler and dropped it into gear, but Penny landed on the gas tank, wedging herself against the ATV and Mila's stomach. "Shir!" She held up a hand as she watched the snowmobiles close in.

"We can't wait. They'll be on him in no time," Mila said, but Penny was insistent.

"Chi chr shee," she explained, and Mila understood her tactic.

She directed Mila to swing in from behind and flank them. That way they could take out a few before they knew what hit them. Mila gripped the handlebars, her thumb twitching to hit the gas. As soon as the last mercenaries' backs were to them, she let loose and rocketed out of the boathouse. The metal cleats on the tires dug in and they were soon catching up to the pack.

The cold wind whipped at Mila's face, making her

squint to see. Unlike the snowmobiles, she had to dodge around occasional drifts of snow. Even then, within seconds, they closed on the tail end of the group.

"Can you hit them?" Mila shouted over her shoulder when they were thirty yards from the last pair.

Danica stood on the foot pegs, leaned on Mila's back, and let loose. The man on the back of the snowmobile crumpled to the side with an arrow between his shoulder blades.

The driver glanced over his shoulder after his passenger fell and saw them. Instead of pulling up his rifle, like Mila expected, he formed a tight bubble of magic in one hand.

Without thinking, Mila drew out the Ivar, took aim, and pulled the trigger.

A bright white streak of energy shot from the gun and sliced through the mercenary before impacting the vehicle and sending it into the air in a flaming wreck.

The pain hit her again, and her vision dimmed, but she shook it off.

"Holy fucking shit, Mila. What the fuck was that?" Danica shouted over the wind and engine noise.

"I think the gun is faulty or something. It keeps taking way more power than it should. My head is killing me."

Penny stared at her.

"What?"

The tiny dragon shook her head.

Mila glanced up to see five of the snowmobiles now coming for them.

Unlike the the last guy, these had guns out and opened fire.

Mila activated her armor before she felt the impacts. The armor made them feel like solid punches but that was it. Behind her, Danica fired another arrow, hitting a driver in the throat. He slumped into the handlebar and sent the vehicle into a roll, throwing both driver and passenger.

Mila veered around a snowdrift and punched the gas.

Penny tapped her on the arm and pointed at the shack. "Chi.Chi."

Mila nodded. "We'll keep them away."

Penny gave her a thumbs-up, then launched into the air and winged toward the little structure.

"Where's she going?" Danica yelled as she let another arrow loose.

"She has to be there when the twins get back so she can overload the rod."

"How do you know that?"

"She told me," Mila shouted before turning hard and sending them into a power slide around another drift.

---

Finn watched as Mila and Danica took out the first snow-mobile. He recognized the magic that came out of Mila's gun and refused to believe it. It was impossible. She would have to be a direct descendent—

A barrage of bullets struck the ice all around him.

He snapped out of his stupor. He figured there were twenty two-man teams on the fast-moving vehicles. He had no chance in a stand-up fight, not out in the middle of a lake anyway. He needed solid ground under him to use effective magic.

Pivoting, Finn ran to the four-wheeler he had detached from the shack earlier and jumped on. He started it, and the chain-covered tires shewed into the ice. He gunned it for the closest shoreline.

Bullets peppered the ice, and a glance over his shoulder told him he was outrunning them, yet still not out of gun range. He swerved in random patterns to make a more difficult target.

Finn was thirty feet from the bank when something hit the back of the ATV and exploded. He flew into the air and into a snowdrift, hitting the ice hard. He rolled to keep from breaking anything and slid at speed toward the snow-covered shore.

A glance revealed the four-wheeler on its side as the pursuers closed in. Finn put a hand to the ice and felt for the magic in the earth. The water was still deep even a few yards from shore, but he kept focused as he slid.

He felt his connection and opened his eyes, which were now gray and full of chilling power. *"Balla cloiche."*

The earth under the frozen water bucked, then a wall of stone erupted through the ice, sending foot-thick ice shards into the air.

The two lead snowmobiles slammed into the wall of rock and exploded in a shower of parts and tumbling bodies.

A snowbank stopped Finn, and he scrambled to his feet. His pursuers had slowed to go around the wall, but were now gunning it his way, some opening fire while three of them shot bubbles that transformed into fireballs.

Finn dove to the side, the fireballs slamming into the

snowdrift behind him, sending up churned ice and earth and gouts of steam.

After scrambling to his feet, Finn ran up the short slope and into the tree cover of the forest. The snow was up to his calves, but his strength pushed him forward at a full run. He went to take cover behind a fallen tree when a bullet ripped through his shoulder and spun him to the ground.

---

Mila whipped around another snowbank and they were on a clear section of the lake, the wind having blown most the snow clear for hundreds of yards around.

"Shit! Danica, take out a few more of these assholes. I don't think I can fire this gun again without passing out."

"On it. Hold steady." She stood and tapped Mila on the head. "Duck." Mila did, and Danica swung her leg over Mila's head so she faced the opposite direction.

The bow let out successive, rapid *thrums* as Danica sent one arrow after another flying. Gunfire answered back, and Mila weaved the vehicle.

"Got one," Danica shouted. A second later added. "Wait, more than one. They're down to three snowmobiles and looks like five guys. Fuck! Turn, turn, turn!"

Mila jammed the handlebars to the left and the spiked tires dug in, sending them up on two wheels. A fireball sizzled past, burning through the space they had just occupied. The flaming ball hit the ice and splashed out in a steaming fan shape, leaving a noticeable divot in the thick ice.

A single snowmobile and driver appeared to their left. He lifted one hand, and Mila saw the telltale sign of a spell forming. He let the bubble fly, and Mila swerved the other way, avoiding the spell and watching it pop into a spray of acid that hissed and spit on the ice.

Danica fired, and Mila couldn't believe they hadn't been shot yet.

"How's it going back there?" Mila shouted as she ramped them over a small drift, then she slid the ATV in a wide loop.

"Good news and bad," Danica shouted. "I took out the caster, but I'm also out of arrows."

"Shit! What are we supposed to do now?" Mila searched for anything that might help them out, but all she saw was open ice.

Danica did the leg over her head thing again to turn back around. She leaned into Mila's ear. "Turn and head straight for them. I have an idea." She held up the stone skin ring.

"What idea, exactly?"

Mila got distracted by a small ball that zipped past her head and skittered in front of them. Her eyes widened and she jerked the handlebars, putting them on two wheels again as she steered.

The grenade exploded and a concussive blast threw the ATV onto all four wheels. The ice bucked as a huge chunk blasted downward, sending a geyser of water into the air. Spiderweb cracks appeared on the ice and more water sprayed up through them.

"Hold on, this is going to be close." Mila dropped a gear and gassed it, speeding them away from the rippling ice.

She was sure they would fall through, but the ATV kept in front of the chain reaction.

"Keep turning! Go right between them," Danica shouted while grasping on to Mila's ribcage so tight it hurt.

"Okay." Mila decided she would get one more shot off. "You go for the right, I'll go for the left."

The gap between them and the snowmobiles closed fast. Mila barely had time to get the pistol up and aimed before Danica leapt off the back of the four-wheeler.

Mila pulled the trigger and a brilliant blast of white magic slammed into the two men on the snowmobile. They exploded. Pain consumed Mila, and she closed her eyes. The sudden odd sensation of flying through the air made her open them. The ATV tumbled away below her in a surreal moment as time slowed and everything came into crisp detail.

Mila must have passed out and lost control, which sent her flying. Below, Danica hurtled toward a snowmobile, her stone skin body tucked into a cannonball. She slammed into the soldiers and crushed them with their own momentum. A cracking sound filled the air, like stone shattering under a hammer, and blood splashed across the ice and snow.

The last thought Mila had was how pretty the bright red looked against the pristine white. Then, she hit the ice and all the colors turned black.

## CHAPTER TWENTY-NINE

D izziness washed over him, and his ears rang.

Finn used his good arm to push himself onto his back. His left arm felt hot, and it hurt to put pressure on it. Glancing over, he saw bright red blood smeared across the fallen tree and soaking the snow around him. It had been long since Finn had been shot. He forgot how shitty it felt.

The roar of snowmobile engines filled the woods and grew louder.

Shaking his head to clear it, Finn reached and unsnapped the compartment on his harness. He withdrew one of his two healing potions. He thumbed the cork free and lifted it to his lips.

"Freeze, asshole!"

A soldier stood less than twenty feet away, his white coat splashed with muddy water. He had his rifle pointed at Finn. "Put the potion down. Now!" The man stepped forward and aimed at Finn's face.

The rage cracked its neck.

Sucking in a deep breath to keep his emotions in check,

Finn stuck the tube of healing potion into the snow, making sure it didn't spill, and raised his good arm.

The man stepped up next to him and kicked the bottle over. "You won't be needing that."

Finn would have let the rage loose and broken the guy's leg, but he needed to be smart. Instead, he dug the fingers of his injured arm into the snow until he felt the pine needle strewn ground…and focused.

"You shouldn't waste healing potions. They're pricey," Finn said with a casual tone.

"You think I give a shit abou—"

"*Spìc cloiche.*"

A stone spike shot from the ground and impaled the man's crotch all the way up and out through his shoulder. He never knew what hit him.

The sound of snowmobiles shutting off told Finn he only had seconds. He pulled out his last healing potion and downed it, sure to get the full dose before tossing the bottle away. He took up Fragar, whispered the power word, and the axe unfolded. Finn got to his feet.

A dozen men on the other side of the fallen tree stared in horror at their impaled comrade, still twitching. Finn let the rage flow. He roared and sprang over the tree.

Two of the mercs formed bubbles of magic. The rest raised their rifles. Finn pushed the rage to its full potential, free from constraints. His vision turned red. His muscles tightened with ferocious power.

Bubbles came at him like missiles, whistling through the air. Finn didn't dodge, relying on his rage to mute their effects. Instead, he launched himself at them. He held Fragar over his head with both arms, the healing potion having fixed his shoulder—or perhaps the rage muted the pain.

At the peak of his jump, the missiles struck him. Fire and acid splashed his body, yet Finn endured no more than a singed beard. He burst from the twin explosions and chopped down on a merc in front of him. It was not a pretty swing, just a savage blow that split the man in two. Gunfire popped all around. Finn ignored it, stepping to the side and chopping the legs out from under a man, then leaping onto the next, smashing his fist into the merc's face and riding him to the ground.

Stronger than he had any right to be, Finn embodied the battle, a blur rendering severed limbs and unleashing animalistic roars. At one point, he pulled someone's arm off and used it as a club, limb in one hand, Fragar in the other.

Trapped inside his own mind while a demon used his body, Finn knew the rage kept him alive. Being this far in the bloodlust was dangerous. Other berserkers got lost in the rage, having to be put down, unable to return from the madness.

Finn recited a mantra. "The rage is in me, but it does not control me." He said it over and over as he slaughtered his enemies. A knife sunk into his thigh. He grabbed the stabber's head in one hand and threw him into another merc, sending them both rolling down a hill. He pulled the knife from his leg and threw it into a third man's chest.

Finn screamed his mantra as he wrenched a rifle from someone, smashing the butt end into the man's neck and breaking his spine.

"The rage is in me, but it does not control me!"

He'd killed at least ten. A dozen still remained, yet several tripped over the dead in their haste to get away from the screaming dwarf. He chased them down and sent them on their way to whatever afterlife would take them.

A set of fireballs hit Finn in the chest. They were as ineffective as the last. He turned and saw the caster had put some distance between them and was forming another set of spells. Finn dropped to one knee, planting the palm of his hand on the ground, and reached for his magic.

To his surprise, it was there.

"*Spìc cloiche.*"

Two factions warred for dominance of his mind. In the end, a spike of stone shot up at an angle and pierced the caster through the heart.

Finn had done it. He had cast a spell while in a full rage. It was a battle, yes, but he had won.

Spinning, he spied five mercs left, three pointing guns at him, two running down the hill, their weapons abandoned. Finn faced off with the three. He growled and tightened his grip on Fragar, then charged, kicking up snow and covering the distance as they opened fire while backpedaling. Most of the shots went wide, although one hit him in the thigh and another below his ribs on his side.

Finn threw Fragar at one of them, then dove onto the second, pressing his palm to the man's face. "*Gunna salainn.*"

A blast of rock salt shot from his palm and tore through the man's skull.

The third man fell backward to get away. He pulled the trigger. The gun clicked empty, and he scrambled to change out the magazine.

Finn pulled a knife from the belt of the man he'd just killed and threw it. It stuck into the last living man's chest, and he became still.

Finn retrieved Fragar, then stumbled on his injured leg. He dare not let the rage recede, not yet. The pain would cripple him, so he stoked the fire while controlling his breathing. A wash of energy gave him the ability to break into a stumbling jog down the hill.

He was a dozen yards from the ice when he stopped and leaned on a tree. He took a second to catch his breath and fix his hold on his rage. Then he looked up, and his heart skipped a beat. Out on the ice, Hellena, her black aura roiling off her pale skin, her delicate face twisted in a snarling visage, held someone by the front of their coat.

Mila. Her limp body like a ragdoll.

Beyond the Dark Star, Finn spotted Danica, her skin and unmistakable hair like white marble, cradling her arm to her chest. An arm that ended at the elbow. Shards of stone were scattered across the ice, along with two bodies that looked like they'd smashed against a wall at high velocity.

"The game is over, Finnegan!" Hellena's voice carried in the still afternoon air. "Come out now, and I won't rip your little friend's head from her shoulders!"

# CHAPTER THIRTY

Penny landed on Finn's shoulder.

"Chi! Shir, shee," she started, then placed a hand on his temple to help tame his rage.

He gently pulled her hand away. "I'm fine. I have it under control," he said, staring at Mila's limp body. "Did the twins get back yet?"

Penny pointed, and he looked to see Regan's and Ronan's heads peeking out of the hut. Between them was the three-foot-long canister containing the fuel rod.

"They got it." He gave a grim smile.

"Chi." Penny gazed at the Dark Star and their two injured friends. "Squee shir?"

Finn thought for a second. "I have to go out there, but we can't let her have the *Anthem*. Go to the shed and over-load the rod. Drop it down the hole. Then, you and the twins make a run for it. I'll get Mila and Danica."

"Chi?"

He growled. "I don't know what I'll do about her. I'll think of something."

She patted his shoulder. "Shir." Penny took to the air and circled back around, staying out of sight.

"Good luck to you, too." Finn took a slow breath and stoked his rage one more time before limping to the shore.

Blood squished in his boot from the knife and bullet wound.

The Dark Star smiled with malice at him. "I knew you couldn't leave her to die. Sentiment gets you every time." She gave Mila a shake.

Finn closed the distance between them slowly. "Let her go, Hellena. I'm the one you want. Let her go, and I'll come with you."

He saw Danica getting to her feet, although she swayed, shaken from the devastating injury. Behind her, a banged-up four-wheeler idled on the snow.

"We are far beyond that now. I told you my people were working to get the Gjallarhorn working; I trust that they can. But I can't trust you. Not after this." She spoke in a normal tone, but magic amplified her voice.

"So what do you want? Give me the girl, and we'll leave. Leave Denver, whatever you want." He kept closing the distance, exaggerating his limp so she might underestimate him. The rage flowed, but he kept it off his face.

She laughed. "I don't care what promises you make. You are far too dangerous to let live. All I want now is for you to watch."

Finn narrowed his eyes. "Watch what?"

"Watch me kill your precious Mila." She held out a hand and it filled with smoke that condensed into a bubble as black as her namesake. "This is the price of insolence, dwarf king." Her face twisted into a mask of hatred. "I told you your refusal would cost your friends' lives. Witness now what you have brought upon yourself!"

Finn broke into a sprint, but he was too far to make it. He cocked his arm back to hurl Fragar when Mila's head rolled forward and her eyes opened.

"Shut the fuck up, bitch." Mila pointed the Ivar at Hellena's face and pulled the trigger. A blast of pure white light enveloped Hellena's head and shoulders. The Dark Star dropped Mila and screamed. She staggered backward and fell to the ice, clutching her face.

Finn didn't stop running, but he changed direction and scooped Mila into his arms. He bounded toward the four-wheeler as Danica climbed into it. "Danica! We need to get the fuck out of here."

She gazed over her shoulder, her elven eyes looking from her stone skin mask and clearing at the sight of him holding Mila. Finn slid to a stop beside the ATV and climbed on the back. He caught a glimpse of Hellena climbing unsteadily to her feet, her face a smoking mess.

The sound of a snowmobile came from their left, and he glanced to see the twins racing across the ice away from the shed with Penny soaring above them.

"Go!" Finn shouted, and Danica hit the gas.

The tires spun, then the metal studs bit in, and they rocketed forward.

Finn glanced back and saw the Dark Star standing, black smoke roiling off of her in thick streams. She raised her hands and the smoke coalesced between them, spinning faster and faster, crackling with bolts of red lightning. Her furious glare met Finn's, her red and blistered face twisted in hatred.

Time slowed, and Finn saw the madness in Hellena's soul. She was smart and capable and able to organize a worldwide movement.

And she was also batshit crazy.

She was going to kill him. She was going to kill them all.

A powerful and low-pitched sound shuddered beneath them, so powerful they could feel it in their bones. It lifted the ice from below. Snowdrifts jumped upward. The lake cracked and echoed from all directions. Finn's chest vibrated as a shockwave passed through him.

The Dark Star held her magic, her expression one of confusion. She gazed at the ice below her. "What have you done?" she screamed, pulling her hands apart and dispelling her magic, only to put them together again to form a new spell.

Too late.

The ice bucked in a dome several hundred yards wide and a good twenty feet high or more. Hellena fell to her knees, her spell disrupted. Then, the dome collapsed, sucked into the lake in a bowl. It sent a wave outward at incredible speed, ripping the ice in boulder-sized chunks. The center of the bowl exploded upward and a geyser of freezing water and ice shot two-hundred feet into the air.

The wave gained on them as it destroyed the surface and sucked everything on the ice into the water. Bodies and snowmobiles disappeared under the wave.

"Faster," Finn called out.

"I have it floored!" Danica protested. "We're almost there."

Finn saw the shore coming quick. It was going to be close.

The foaming ice-filled mini-tsunami roared only a few yards behind them.

"Hang on!" Danica warned before they hit the shore.

The ATV jarred them forward as they smashed into the slope, and the wave slammed into the back of the four-wheeler, hammering a couple chunks of ice into Finn's back and flung him off the vehicle. He tucked Mila into him as they hit the ground and rolled. They came to a stop, ice and slush washing over them.

Then, all was still. Finn wiped the freezing water off his face, and saw Mila was soaked and still unconscious in his arms. "We need to get her inside."

Danica climbed off the ATV and stumbled around piles of ice all across the yard.

Finn struggled to his feet and staggered to her side, Mila still cradled in his arms. "Put your arm around my neck," he said, leaning into Danica.

She wrapped a stone arm over his shoulders with a quiet groan, and they made their way toward the house. They came across the twins and Penny laying on the ground, catching their breath.

"Help her," Finn ordered, and the two selkies jumped up and took Danica's considerable weight between them.

Finn led them up the steps, and Penny opened the door.

He stopped and gave her a nod. "Good work, Pen. You saved our asses with that overload."

She gave him a guilty look. "Chir shee."

"Ten minutes?" he raised an eyebrow. "It was less than two."

"Chi chi." She shrugged.

He chuckled. "Yeah, you *did* say it was unpredictable. Let's get a fire going and see what we can do for the girls."

"Shir shee chir." Penny led the way inside.

Finn gazed out at the broken, oscillating waters. "I don't think so, Penny. We'll see her again."

## CHAPTER THIRTY-ONE

Finn laid Mila on the couch, and Regan began stripping Mila's wet, frozen clothes off while Penny and Ronan built up a fire in the fireplace. With Regan taking over care for Mila, Finn went to Danica, who was leaning against the kitchen island and still wore her soaked, bloodstained coat. She held her broken-off appendage close to her chest.

"Dan..." He cleared his throat and put a hand on her shoulder. "Let's get this off you and have a look."

She nodded and let him do it, her marble cheeks wet from the wave or tears or both. They got the bloody garment off. He tossed it in the sink, and pulled out a pocketknife, wincing when he dug his hand into the pocket of his wounded leg. Danica snapped from her stupor when she noticed he was in pain.

Her eyes went wide. "Finn! Why didn't you say you were hurt?" She began to reach for his harness with her broken arm and stopped, switching to her left hand, and searched for his potions.

"What happened to your potions?"

He gave her a weak smile and opened the pocketknife. "Used 'em. I was hoping you could stitch me up when we get one of Mila's into you." He grabbed the long sleeve of her shirt that hung over the stump and cut it off, exposing the rough break where her forearm had been.

She glanced at it and sniffed back tears. "I can't..." she said with a hoarse voice. "It's...gone."

"That's what the potion is for."

She shook her head. "You don't understand. As soon as I take the ring off, my arm will be gone. Forever. I need the stones that made it up to get it back, but they're at the bottom of the lake."

Finn's face fell. "These potions have grown limbs back before."

She laughed and sobbed at the same time. "This is different. The ring changes you at a cellular level. When I take it off, it'll change me back...minus my arm. My body will think I'm not supposed to have one, so a healing potion won't regrow it. It's why these rings are so risky."

She held up her good hand with the ring on her middle finger. "Would you mind? I'm shorthanded at the moment."

"Really? A joke?" Finn took her hand in his.

She sniffed. "Laughter is the best medicine or so I've heard. Please. Take it off. It'll be okay. We'll figure something out."

He frowned then reached up and slipped the ring off her finger. Her skin and hair began to gain color. It was odd to see her hair turn deep brown.

"Your hair." He held out a strand.

She laughed and sniffed. "I told you I dye it."

They avoided glancing at her arm.

"I'm sorry. I shouldn't have asked you to come," he said.

She gave him a sad smile. "I wouldn't have missed it for the world. Besides, it wasn't like I could have stayed home with assassins crawling all over the place. Don't feel sorry for me. I'm the only person I know who can say they would give their right arm to help their friends and mean it."

He chuckled, and they both peered down to see a healed stump three inches below her elbow.

"At least it isn't bleeding," she said. She looked at him. "Now your turn. Since you've already drank a potion today, we should hold off giving you another for a few hours. Take your pants off, and let's look at your leg."

He did as asked and sat up on the kitchen island. Danica began washing the blood away with a clean dish towel and water. "I would use sterile pads to clean this, but we'll have you take a potion anyway in a couple hours. Right now, we can't have you losing blood like a sieve, so I'll glue it." She held up a bottle of super glue procured from one of the kitchen drawers.

"Why not stitch it?" Then he felt foolish for asking.

"Well, besides the obvious, I can't stitch the muscle one-armed, but we need to keep it closed. You got lucky. No major arteries were opened."

She called Ronan over and had him hold Finn's wounds together while she applied a thin layer of glue and sealed the edges together. Afterward, Danica went to the fridge and pulled out a beer.

She stared at the bottle, realizing she couldn't open it,

and tears sprang into her eyes. Finn hobbled to her side and opened it.

"I suppose I'll need to learn to use a prosthetic. I saw they have robotic ones at my last conference. Maybe I'll get one of those."

That gave Finn an idea. "Holy shit. A prosthetic. That's it. We can get you a dwarven-made one. I'll bet the Huldu have some in stock from the original voyage."

Danica shook her head. "Why would dwarves make prosthetics? That's such a niche thing for something like this." She held up her stump.

"Not all races can use healing potions. The empire is huge. There's a demand for everything out there."

"A dwarven-made arm would be bad-ass," Ronan cut in.

She peered at the selkie and half-smiled, then turned her gaze back to Finn. "Are dwarven prosthetics bad-ass?" she asked, her mood lightening.

He gave her a sly smile. "Oh, you'll see."

---

An hour later, Hermin appeared in a bubble, his face red with anger.

They all wore dry clothes and huddled on the couches beside the fire. The twins played their game, this time with headphones on. Finn had Mila cradled on his lap, wrapped in a thick blanket, and Penny rested on top of it. Danica was under her own blanket, resting her head against Finn's shoulder.

Hermin glared at them. "What the hell, people? I said keep it low-key and you go and set off a magical explosion so powerful we felt it all the way in Denver. How is that low-key?"

Finn gave him a smile. "Oh, hey, Hermin. Sorry. It wasn't like we were planning on facing off with Hellena. It just sort of happened."

Hermin pulled on his hair with both hands and made a noise before sputtering, "Just sort of happened? We have to erase everyone's memories for twenty miles! Do you know how much time that'll take? And who the heck is Hellena?"

"The Dark Star." Danica lifted her stump in the air. "I lost an arm." She took a drink of beer.

"You lost…you…your arm? Are you drunk?"

She nodded her heavy head. "Maybe. Don't judge me." She displayed her stump again. "I lost an arm."

"Oh, speaking of," Finn said, "Any chance there are dwarven prosthetics in the cargo holds? I kinda promised to get one for her."

Hermin was so flustered he couldn't speak for a few seconds. Finally, he sighed. "I'll check. There were some a few thousand years ago, and I don't know why anyone would have taken them. Give me a few days on that. Look. There's going to be a lot of cleaning up here. Can you guys do me one favor?"

"Sure, you name it Hermin," Finn answered.

"Please, for the love of god, don't blow any more shit up for, like, at least a month. Can you do that?"

Finn bit his lip and furrowed his brow. "I promise we'll do our best."

Hermin nodded. "I thought you might say something like that. Okay, I'll be around for the next few days if you need anything. And, I'll look into the prosthetic."

"Thanks, Hermin. I owe you one," Finn said.

Hermin gave him a hard stare. "Considering this, I think it's a few more than one." He formed a bubble around himself and disappeared.

―――――――――

Finn's head snapped up. The fire had burned down to glowing embers, casting the room in dark red. The twins and Danica had gone to bed already, and Penny was curled up and snoring on Mila's chest.

Mila still slept, using his lap as a pillow. He heard an intermittent buzzing sound and peered around the living room. Finn gently moved out from under Mila and replaced his leg with a pillow. After some searching, he found it was his discarded, bloody pants making the noise. He reached into a pocket and found his phone, which had been switched to vibrate. The caller ID read 'restricted.'

Finn hit the answer button. "Hello?"

A raspy female voice accosted him, "Finnegan. So nice to hear your voice again."

"Hellena," he growled. "Can't say the same about you."

She laughed, which turned into a cough for several seconds. "I must say, I'm impressed you hid your little friend's true nature from me for so long. Had I realized there were any Valkyries left on Earth, I would have recruited her long ago."

"Valkyrie..." Finn started, then it all fell into place. Mila's affinity for nature manifested in her ability to communicate with insects, her unnatural luck for winning fights no anthropologist should win, and her obsession with speed. All those things and more. She had channeled celestial power through the Ivar pistol!

Mila was a fucking Valkyrie.

"Oh, you didn't know?" Hellena's voice sounded gravelly and tired yet still had its usual air. "How interesting."

"I suppose this is another threat then? More bounties, more men coming after us? But, let me guess, this time it's personal and all that shit? Well, let me tell you something, Hellena. More people in more star systems than you can count have threatened me and guess what? Most of them make you look like nothing more than a schoolyard bully. You can take your fucking dark star shit and shove it up your ass. You are *not* coming for me, motherfucker, I'm coming for *you*."

She hummed with joy. "Oh, I knew you would be something special, dwarf king. I welcome the challenge. I was calling to tell you that, yes, this *is* personal now. But I have canceled the bounties on your heads." Her tone shifted. "Because I intend to kill you myself."

"Well, I hope you bring your diapers then."

"My...diapers? What are you talking about?"

"Because I'm going to beat the shit out of you." He laughed and ended the call.

"Who was that?" Mila asked, gazing sleepily over the back of the couch.

He smiled. "You're up."

She nodded, then groaned. "My head is killing me, but I think I'll be okay." She squinted at him in the dark. "Was it Hellena?"

"Yeah. Bad news, she's still alive. Good news, she canceled the bounties."

Mila brightened. "That *is* good."

"I guess. The downside is she's coming after us herself." He set the phone on the table and crossed his arms. "But you put a damn good hurt on her, so I think we have time before she's in fighting shape again."

"Good. Then you can take me on that date." She smiled.

He laughed. "Okay. When?"

"Right now." She pointed at the hot tub outside. "Grab some beers. I'll meet you out there."

He smiled, then his expression fell. "There's a lot we need to talk about."

She held up a hand. "Is anyone dead?"

He shook his head.

"Is anyone going to die?"

He shook his head again.

"Then we can talk about it in the morning." She stood with the blanket wrapped around her. "Give me five minutes and I'll be out. Don't forget the beers."

He held his hands up in surrender. "Okay. You win. I'll grab the beers."

She padded down the hall and disappeared into one of the bedrooms.

Finn pushed off the table and walked to the fridge. Danica must have been planning on partying when she went to the store earlier. It was stocked despite the ones they'd already drank. He grabbed six bottles and carried them to the balcony door, then awkwardly opened it with his elbow.

It was snowing again. He crunched through two fresh inches of it and set the beers on a snow-covered table beside the built-in hot tub. He made a clear spot in the snow on the deck beside the steaming pool and kicked his boots off then pulled his shirt and pants off and stepped into the water. Finn sucked in a breath at the sudden change in temperature.

He opened two beers, waded to the other side of the tub, and pressed a finger on the dark touchscreen, which lit up to show the controls. He turned on the lights around the rim and liked how they gave a soft glow bright enough to see the people around you. yet not so bright you couldn't see the stars. Another button and the whole tub started bubbling as if full of seltzer water. Satisfied, he turned to find a seat and froze.

Mila stood at the edge of the pool with a pile of towels at her feet. She shivered, but remained standing.

"I didn't think you would ever turn around." She clutched her hands between her breasts to keep warm.

"Why didn't you get in?"

"Because I wanted you to see the suit Danica gave me, dummy. What do you think?"

Mila wore a burnt orange bikini that left little to the imagination. She curtsied.

"It's...amazing. You're amazing," he said.

She hurried into the steaming water and lowered until she was up to her chin. She smiled, just a floating head in the warm, frothy water. "I'm glad you like it, but next time I'm standing practically naked outside in a snowfall, hurry with the compliments. I don't think I have enough meat on me to take the cold as long as it takes you to get a clue."

He laughed and handed her his beer, then went to the table and got one for himself. He sat on the shelf seat that ran around the pool, his chest and shoulders out of the water, and took a long drink as he watched Mila float up onto her back and stare at the stars.

"What was it like up there?" she asked.

He squinted at the stars, appreciating how clear the night sky was up in the mountains and far from the city lights. He sucked in a long breath. "Mostly lonely."

She dropped her feet to the bottom and gave him a long look. "Really?"

"Well, space is big. Like, really fucking big. Something that big can't have a lot of stuff in it. And it always wants to kill you. One slip up and you don't have oxygen or you're irradiated or frozen solid in the dead of space. You spend all your time in a ship, seeing the same walls, smelling the same smells. You go to planets where it's all the same with beings trying to get the better of you or toxic environments, literal, political, or both. Some places are just a dump and all you want to do is get back on your ship and go somewhere else. So...you do. And it takes a long time, because it's all so fucking big, so you're alone some more."

She took a sip of beer, her head the only thing above water. "Are you going to miss it?"

"Maybe."

She slowly walked toward him, her head never rising above the surface. She reminded him of a gator stalking its prey near the shore. Mila stopped in front of him, bobbing up and down and looking him in the eye.

They stayed like that for a full minute, staring at one another, lost in the moment.

She broke the silence. "I'm something weird, aren't I?"

Finn's brows rose before he snorted a chuckle. He took

a long drink of his beer then set it on the tub's edge before glancing back at her.

"I overheard part of what you were saying to Hellena. Is it bad?"

He shook his head. "No."

"Good. Then you can tell me tomorrow." She stood, water dripping down her body, then she wrapped her arms around his neck and kissed him in a way that stole his breath. They kissed a long time after that, enjoying the feel of one another.

She pulled her knees up and sat on his lap, facing him. Her eyes widened. "Finn. Uh…are you naked?"

The dwarf cocked his head at her. "Why would I wear clothes in a tub?"


The End


Coming soon to Amazon and Kindle Unlimited, *Triumph Of The Dwarf King*, Book four in the Finnegan Dragonbender series!

Get sneak peeks, exclusive giveaways, behind the scenes content, and more.
PLUS you'll be notified of special **one day only fan pricing** on new releases.

Sign up today to get free stories.

CLICK HERE

or visit: https://marthacarr.com/read-free-stories/

Up until about four months ago I did 80% of my writing at a place called Western Collective here in my city of Boise. It is a fantastic Brewery/Coffee House, and the best part is that it opens at 7:00am every day. I would go in and get a coffee, then graduate to a beer after lunch. The staff are fantastic, and everyone there knows my name.

When me and my wife moved to Boise the first people we met were our neighbors. We were downtown, sitting outside in one of the plazas, when this guy with a scruffy beard and cowboy hat and a striking blonde came up to us with their two dogs. We had been in town for less than a day at that point.

"Hey, this might sound weird, but I think we're your neighbors." He said, with a handshake. "I saw you through the window." He gave a laugh.

We chatted for a second then he mentioned that he owned Western Collective, and for us to come down and say hi.

So, we did. And now, most of the people me and my

wife consider friends here in Boise either work there or we met them through some function of that place. It was like a nice little second home where two people, new to a city, could go and feel welcome with strangers.

Oh, I almost forgot to mention, Western was less than a mile from our house, so we could walk or bike there in less than five minutes. It was staggeringly convenient.

But, four months ago me and my wife bought a house. It's pretty close to a dream house, and we find ourselves looking around and saying stupid things like, "I can't believe this is our house", or "we actually own this!". Suffice it to say, we love our new house.

The only problem is that it's five miles further away from Western. Five miles doesn't sound like a lot, and it really isn't, but those five miles are through the city, so it's now a good twenty to thirty minute drive depending on traffic.

That's just long enough to be inconvenient. So, I have given up my daily ritual, and now I work from home, in my office, surrounded by my cats, and the warm fuzzy feeling a new house gives you. And it's good.

But…

I find that life is like that sometimes; trade one thing for another. I'm more productive at home, I spend way less money at home, and my cats aren't lonely. (not that they care all that much. They sleep most of the time anyway, the lazy bastards.) However, I have lost the daily social interactions that keep me from becoming a straggly haired monster who talks to himself too much; also known as a professional author.

It's all give and take.

So, today I'm sitting in my beautiful office, the cool winter sun shinning through the window, and a fire roaring in the fireplace. Tomorrow? I think I'll head down to Western and say hi to a few old friends.

Because while it is all give and take, it's also what you make of it. And, I didn't buy a car so I would never leave my house.

I hope these notes find you well, and remind you that you are not a captive of your circumstances. Go out and say hello to some old friends. Trust me, it'll be worth it.

All my best,
Charley Case
Boise, ID

Jennifer Hendricks is the good buddy who'll come play with you and leave just in time so someone's still around to bail out the group later. She's in on every joke and despite her answer to question #2 is willing to be good friends and even hang out with the likes of me, Ramy Vance, and a few Scots I know (we're very respectful, it's those two other things... YTT LIVES!). Long after I've gone home for the night I still see pictures on Facebook of the gang still hanging, and there's Jennifer right in the mix. The bail money would come later...

She is not only a rising star as an author (check her out if you like clean romance or sci-fi), but one of the go-to's behind the scenes at LMBPN if you want the cogs to actually turn in a timely fashion. That's a giant job that takes the skills of a diplomat.

These days there are a lot of authors publishing under the LMBPN flag (Have we hit a hundred yet?) and everyone has requests, big and small and Jennifer handles all of it with grace and speed, and manages to steer the occasional lost lamb of an author back on course. Occasionally that's even me.

All of that while writing her own series and being good natured about it. Makes it a great place to collaborate and get things done and just adds to the phrase, dream job.

**1. What turns you on?**

Good manners. Gentlemen who open doors and respect women.

**2. What turns you off?**

Cussing, crudeness, lack of respect.

**3. Who do you most admire? Why?**

Indie authors in general. They took such a huge leap of faith and self-published their own books. They are doing it all and for the most part don't rely on anyone else to do their work for them. It is a TON of work to write, publish, and market your own book. Kudos to all of them!

**4. What profession other than your own would you like to attempt?**

I've always wanted to be a working actor. I've been in 1 movie as an extra and one episode of a reality tv show that was only on 1 season. I don't need to be a star, just work enough to support myself.

**5. What profession would you not like to do?**

Politics. LOL When I was young I wanted to be the first female President of the USA. I'm so glad I changed my mind a long time ago. LOL

**6. If heaven exists, what would you like to hear God say when you arrive at the pearly gates?**

Welcome, my good and faithful servant.

**7. What is your favorite movie?**

OH, this is tough. Almost all of the Hallmark movies

would qualify. LOL But If I could only choose 1, it would probably be the 5 hour BBC version of Pride and Prejudice.

**8. Who is your favorite character and from what book by which author?**

Mr. Darcy from Pride and Prejudice (Jane Austen), but I also have a thing for Four from Divergent (Veronica Roth)

**9. What is something most people do not know about you?**

I speak Russian and have traveled to Russia multiple times, including to Siberia and Sochi.

**10. What do you look forward to most in the new year?**

Finding a new place to live. I just sold my condo and am staying with family. I really need my own place again. LOL.

**11. What's your favorite non-LMBPN series you've done? What's your favorite series inside LMBPN?**

Favorite non-LMBPN Series I've written is Miss Claus.

Favorite series within LMBPN is yet to be released.

Do you have a web site you'd like to promote? If so, leave the link for me.

https://jlhendricksauthor.com/

**If smart phones and GPS rule the world - why am I hunting a magic compass to save the planet?**

Austin Detective Maggie Parker has seen some weird things in her day, but finding a surly gnome rooting through her garage beats all.

Her world is about to be turned upside down in a frantic search for 4 Elementals.

Each one has an artifact that can keep the Earth humming along, but they need her to unite them first.

Unless the forces against her get there first.

<u>**AVAILABLE ON AMAZON AND IN KINDLE UNLIMITED!**</u>

# OTHER BOOKS IN THE TERRANAVIS UNIVERSE

The Adventures of Maggie Parker Series

The Witches of Pressler Street

Other books by Martha Carr

Other books by Charley Case

## JOIN THE TERRANAVIS UNIVERSE FACEBOOK GROUP

## FOLLOW TERRANAVIS UNIVERSE ON FACEBOOK

www.ingramcontent.com/pod-product-compliance
Lightning Source LLC
Chambersburg PA
CBHW050248110726
47898CB00007B/2325

* 9 7 8 1 6 4 2 0 2 6 9 8 6 *